I0822439

VOLUME ONE

BOOK TWO

THE SECOND SIGN

BY

DWAYNE ANTHONY MADRY

Printed in the United States of America

First Printing, 2024

ISBN 978-1-963089-01-1

Cover Design by JessHavok

www.SAHAEL.com

Intoduction into Sahael

As Oadira flees the estate amidst the chaos of rebellion, Madame Lalaurie becomes aware of her escape and is determined to recapture her prized investment. With the entire estate on high alert, overseers and catchers are dispatched to track down Oadira, intensifying the search for the elusive princess.

Desperate to evade capture, Oadira taps into her magical abilities, using them voluntarily for the first time to outwit her pursuers. The young princess employs all her skills and instincts to stay ahead of those hunting her, navigating through the tumultuous events unfolding around her.

As Oadira's flight takes her towards the outer island of Iceoth, a remarkable phenomenon occurs. The waters surrounding her begin to change, responding to her presence in a startling display of power. With a mesmerizing gaze, Oadira's brown eyes seem to communicate with the turbulent blue waters, invoking a forceful intervention that thwarts the ships pursuing her, creating a barrier that pushes them back against the relentless tide.

The unexpected manifestation of Oadira's connection to the elements hints at the depths of her latent powers and the profound impact she may have on the world around her. As she continues her journey towards the sanctuary of Iceoth, the significance of her abilities and her role in the unfolding events becomes increasingly apparent, setting the stage for a destiny that transcends the boundaries of her known existence.

Chapter CONTENTS

CHAPTER I

THE PLAN

Lucedale Colony, Lalaurie Estate

Three months after the Royal Rumble, Madame Lalaurie became curious about Oadira's pregnancy.

Or more appropriately, her lack of a pregnancy.

Nezikiah and his trainer Solomon had visited Oadira first, before traveling to see Aamira and Heziara. Within days of the Royal Rumble, Solomon had arrived and secretly begun Oadira's training. The hours Madame Lalaurie assumed Oadira was spending being impregnated by Nezikiah, she was in fact being trained in how to use her magic artes by Solomon. No breeding had taken place at all. Now, two months after they had left the first time, Solomon had returned for another round, but Madame Lalaurie was apparently growing impatient.

"Madame Lalaurie is suspicious," Oadira said as she sat across from Solomon in the breeding suite on the south end of the plantation house. A large bed anchored the room with fine linens spread across it. A sitting area with couches and chairs were arranged next to a window that gazed out on the orchards where slave labor pruned branches and raked fallen leaves. Nezikiah stood near the door, silent as always, muscular arms held behind his back like a guard on watch.

It would have been a comfortable room if not for the unsavory nature of its purpose.

"I overheard her last night, speaking with Mr. Plummer, the overseer," Oadira continued as Solomon took a sip of tea from a porcelain cup. "She thinks I should be pregnant after your first visit. She's expecting my belly to start showing in the next several days. It's time to put our plan into action."

"Pregnancy doesn't happen immediately in every case," Solomon assured. "For some couples it takes years of trying to conceive. I will speak with Madame Lalaurie about this if you would like."

"It's not Madame Lalaurie I'm worried about," Oadira said, tapping her finger against the couch upholstery. "She's hired a new overseer; a reincarnation of a witan devil if you ask me. Plummer is suspicious of everything. He stares at my eyes when we're in the house together. He's always asking about my movements and where I go when I'm not in my room. I think the Madame hired him just to make sure I get pregnant and don't run off once I have the baby."

"This may make escaping more difficult for you," Solomon said, rubbing his eyebrow. "What can you tell me about this Mr. Plummer?"

"He's pudgy, stinky, and sweaty," Oadira grimaced. "He has yellow missing teeth and a meanness that rivals the Madame's sister Martha. He's a miserable drunkard, profane swearer, and a savage monster. He's always armed with a cowskin whip and a heavy cudgel. Just yesterday, I saw him cut and slash a woman's head so horribly that even Madame Lalaurie was enraged at his cruelty and threatened to whip him if he did it to any other slaves,"

“He sounds like all witans. He’s just not hiding his true colors,” Solomon said, taking another sip of tea. “The White Darkness has pierced Mr. Plummer’s red, beating heart, suffocating it with hate, anger, and self-pity. I was hoping for a few more days with you, but this news disturbs me. I believe your worries are justified. A man such as this is here for one purpose: to guard the Madame’s assets; you and whatever child you may have. And at this point, any baby of Nezikiah the champion wrestler will be worth more than you are. He will brutalize you if he thinks it necessary or thinks you will run away once pregnant. His vigilance will only increase. Your time may have arrived ahead of schedule. How goes your training since we left?”

The training. While arduous and sometimes boring even, Oadira had grown to love the moments sitting alone, expanding her senses and control over her environment. Just the week before she had finally linked minds with Constance, a pet goldfish swimming in a bowl beside the Madame’s bed. She had watched Lalaurie writing a letter and yelling at Amahlé to bring her some butter and crackers from the cellar. To imagine being able to see through the eyes of all marine animals excited Oadira to no end. She had also become more skilled in reading emotions, feeling the excitement of the plantation slaves even now for the mere possibility of liberation.

“It’s going alright,” Oadira admitted. “But I need more time with you.”

“I doubt you’ll have it. You must go now, within the next few days, and ignite the embers of rebellion that will destroy this plantation and the nautical slave trade that runs through the Lalaurie’s estates in the three colonies. When is the next ship leaving for Iceoth?”

“Tomorrow morning from Dock 7, according to the manifests Madame Lalaurie has in her study.”

Solomon rubbed his chin. “Tomorrow morning. Can you get things moving that quickly?”

“I can,” Oadira said confidently, though her heart suddenly beat faster.

“Have you made copies of the Madame’s maps and memorized every location on the estate?”

“I have.”

“Good.” Solomon stood, motioning for Oadira to do the same. He embraced her. His green robes seemed to envelope her in a feeling of comfort and safety. She had grown to love Solomon even though their mentorship had been necessarily brief. “It’s time for me to leave,” he whispered, breaking their hug. “This is the last time you and I will see each other. I arranged for both Aamira and Heziara to be at the Vannadale mansion when Nezikiah and I arrive in a few days. That will give me time to instruct them on their own escapes before the news of your flight reaches the Lalaurie sisters. Are you ready to do this?”

“Yes, everything is in place.”

“And the slaves here on the plantation?”

“I’ve been spreading the word since we returned from the Royal Rumble. Amahlé has been helping me. All that is needed are the spirituals to awaken the Diaspora who are on standby, waiting for their signals. The Madame will be leaving this evening and returning late at night to sleep. From there, she’ll go off to the imperial city sometime tomorrow for a meeting with the barons.”

“Wonderful. It’s time for me to go,” Solomon said, snapping his fingers toward Nezikiah, who nodded in response. “Remember to take the maps and instructions I’ve left for you regarding the gates and such in Iceoth. My instructions won’t make sense until you’re there, so keep them close.”

“Will I see you again?” Oadira asked. Solomon said this

would be the last time they'd see each other, but Oadira hoped beyond reason that wasn't a statement of fact.

A knock at the door paused their conversation. Amahlé entered, carrying a tray of food and wine. She looked tired, but energized, the wrinkles around her brown eyes more pronounced than usual.

"You two have been talking long enough," Amahlé said, placing the tray on the coffee table next to the couch. "You need to run along, Solomon, before Mr. Plummer starts thinking you're the one impregnating Oadira. We have to keep up the proper ruse, do we not?"

"That we do, Amahlé," Solomon smiled. He grabbed a piece of cheese from the platter and took a bite. "I appreciate your candor and your timing." He turned to Oadira. "Amahlé and I will leave you and Nezikiah to your performance. As to your question…trust in Ishtar, Obatala, and all the Gods of Sahael. None of us know what tomorrow brings. Have faith and look to the shores of Sahael for our people's salvation."

Oadira nodded, holding back tears. After Solomon and Amahlé left and closed the door behind them, she and Nezikiah broke out into a chorus of fake moaning, ensuring any eavesdroppers would report the performance of their sexual activities straight to Madame Lalaurie. Oadira had to make a concerted effort not to burst out laughing as Nezikiah's face contorted each time he grunted. Having his tongue removed by the slavers hadn't affected Nezikiah's ability to be humorous when he wanted to.

After a few hours, Princess Amahlé and Nezikiah emerged from her room. Solomon and Nezikiah were escorted off the estate, perhaps never to be seen by Oadira again. She stood in the afternoon sunlight as the carriage moved down the gravel path toward the main road. A bit of sweat trickled down the back of her neck, but it wasn't because of the humidity.

"Are you okay?" Amahlé asked.

"I'm fine," Princess Oadira said.

Amahlé motioned toward the trees and the grassy field beyond. "Let's go on our midday walk in the fresh air. The spirituals need to be sung, and we must keep up appearances so as to not bring any suspicions down on us."

Several minutes into their walk, Amahlé and Princess Oadira frowned at the unpleasantness plaguing Madame Lalaurie's estate. A group of witan overseers were punishing a new crop of slaves using the Sisyphus method—forcing them to drag a five-ton obsidian boulder across the entire plantation. Others were being pushed into cramped boxes and buried with only small holes for air. They would barely have enough oxygen to breathe, only to be released hours later weak and confused. Oadira took a step toward them, but Amahlé grabbed her wrist.

"There's nothing we can do for them right now," Amahlé whispered.

"We need to get the maps to the people in the slave quarters, so that they can be distributed among everyone," Oadira replied. "Solomon said the time is now. We can't wait any longer."

"Then all we can do is sing the song of escape," Educator Amahlé said. "Do you think the people are ready? Are you ready?"

Oadira watched one of the slaves being slapped by a shorter witan man. "We've been ready for 15 years," Oadira spat.

"Very well." Amahlé took a deep breath, vibrating her vocal cords. She began to sing. While older and bent with age and toil, her voice rang strong and melodic through the trees. *"We've been bucked, and we've been scorned. We've been talked about sure's you're born."*

Suddenly, about a quarter of the people in the slave quarters started singing the chorus in unison. Even the men being forced into the boxes shouted out with surprising strength.

"But we'll never turn back. No, we'll never turn back until we've all been free, and we have equality."

The witan slavers looked around; confusion written in the lines on their pale faces. One of the overseers whipped a large Sahaelian dragging the stone and screamed for him to shut up. The slave continued singing even louder.

Amahlé started the second verse, her beautiful voice echoing around the estate. *"We have walked thru the shadows of death. We've had to walk all by ourselves."*

This time, not a single slave remained quiet. It was as if the ground itself came to life and the voices of the dead added volume to the chorus.

"But we'll never turn back. No, we'll never turn back until we've all been free, and we have equality."

Amahlé smiled as she and Oadira continued walking. The third verse began even louder as Amahlé added passion to her words. *"We have served our time in jail, with no money for to go our bail."*

The trees themselves seemed to sing with the voices of the oppressed. *"But we'll never turn back. No, we'll never turn back until we've all been free, and we have equality."*

Then Amahlé sang the last verse, looking at Oadira. *"We have hung our heads and cried for those like us who've died, died for you and died for me. Died for the cause of equality."*

The entire slave quarter started singing. *"But we'll never turn back. No, we'll never turn back until we've all been free, and we have equality."*

The witan overseers looked back at Amahlé, and then turned their backs to those singing the song of escape, not knowing at all what it meant. The overseers would likely be hung from Madame Lalaurie's hanging tree by Mr. Plummer for not stopping the singing. Oadira felt no sadness at the thought. Too bad even Plummer had no idea what this song would lead to.

Tonight, these slave men would break the backs of their tormentors. Tonight, they would breathe free air.

"The spark has been lit.," Amahlé said. "Let us continue to walk and move through the Estate as usual. Where are we off to next?"

"The breeding farms and the brothels," Oadira said. "Everyone needs to hear the song. Everyone needs to be given hope." She kicked a rock and sent it tumbling into the grass. "Everyone needs to know that tonight we fight back. For Sahael."

After several miles, Amahlé and Princess Oadira came upon the breeding farm. The line of shacks ran along the road, smelling of sweat and mud. A long line of witan men and women waited out front for their turn to have intercourse with enslaved men, women, and even children. Not only was this a way for Madame Lalaurie to make money from the transient workers passing through the area who were willing to pay for a physical release, but it allowed her to add to her slave counts since even half-blood children were still not counted as a person and thus could be put into the fields as soon as they were old enough to work. Newborn babies were taken from their mothers the moment they leave their wombs, trained to be slaves their entire lives. Many of them would die from malnourishment and exposure before they reached adulthood.

As they walked past the line of waiting predators, Amahlé started singing the second spiritual. *"Keep your eyes on the prize. Keep your eyes on the prize. Keep your eyes on the prize."*

Amahlé's voice rang loudly, seeping through the walls of the brothels and breeding farms entering the minds of the men, women, and children being violated. After hearing Amahlé's voice, the women in the birthing houses started singing the chorus.

"Hold on, hold on, keep your eyes on the prize. Hold on, hold on." The mothers sang in unison from Madame Lalaurie's birthing center, forcing the witan midwives to pause and listen.

"Nauz and Sam, bound in jail, bed no money for to go their bail," Amahlé sang.

"Keep your eyes on the prize, hold on, hold on," came the response.

The witans in the long lines for the brothels paused and listened to the rising chorus of voices. Some of the men tapped their feet, as if the song was somehow for their benefit.

"The only thing we did wrong, stayed in the wilderness a day too long," Amahlé sang as Princess Oadira joined for the last verse.

"But the one thing we did right was the day we started fighting," sang the people in the breeding farms and brothels.

Oadira and Amahlé continued walking without looking back. For the past two months, the women on the breeding farms had hidden knives under their mattresses, waiting for the signal.

The signal had now been given.

Tonight, they would fight back. Tonight, many of their oppressors would die.

The chorus repeated as Oadira and Amahlé continued walking down the road. "The message has been received and accepted," Oadira nodded. She rubbed her fingers together, shaking slightly. "There will be much death before the sun sets today. I don't welcome it."

“Welcome the freedom our people deserve,” Amahlé said.

“I do, but the women in the breeding farms are going to kill all witan midwives and their babies.”

“Yes,” Amahlé continued, looking up as they stepped from the shade of a grove of trees into the bright sunlight. “Freeing them from the hell they were born into. We didn’t start this, but it comes to us to finish it. Let’s hurry and get to the Madame’s laboratories and meet those who have heard the three spirituals in the barn. Plummer will have gotten word about the singing by now. The man’s not an idiot. He’ll know something is up.”

Amahlé and Princess Oadira approached the Madame’s laboratories and barn. Unlike the dilapidated breeding shacks, these buildings were well kept and painted. The red barn with its while lattice work made one think of prosperity and abundance, even though inside people were tortured and mutilated to satisfy the curiosity of witan ‘scientists.’ Oadira had snuck out here at night before, but couldn’t stand to watch too closely or for too long at the pain of her people. Even now, in the shining sunlight of a spring day, she wanted to shut her eyes to the suffering and run away.

Normally a set of four guards patrolled the perimeter between the two buildings, but today, all was quiet.

“There are no guards outside the Madame’s labs,” Oadira noticed.

“There won’t be today,” Amahlé smiled. “While you and Nezikiah were performing, I sent word quickly to the servants. Each of the guards was offered a free session at the breeding pens. Apparently, they ran off an hour ago and have been entertained ever since.”

It was a good strategy, Oadira admitted, though the thought of her slave sisters being forced to pleasure such men made her stomach twist. It seemed no matter what they did, someone suffered for it.

After today, the witan oppressors would finally feel that same suffering.

"We need to get to the barn," Oadira said, walking faster. "There are many waiting for us who have heard the first two songs of rebellion; they await the final spiritual."

They arrived just outside the barn and could hear the obsidian chains clinking against each other as the enslaved waited for their arrival. Oadira peaked through one of the dirty windows, seeing little through the darkness beside several men standing chained nearby, including three young boys no older than ten.

"The Madame said that she doesn't use children in her 'research,'" Princess Oadira said, recalling a past conversation with Madame Lalaurie where she extolled her virtues as a slave owner and how merciful she was, particularly to the children of her charges.

"Do you believe everything witan's say?" Amahlé asked.

"No," Oadira answered.

"Good. Don't start now. Witans tell you what you want to hear. It's how they control and manipulate you. Witans go out of their way to turn you against your own people, dividing and conquering and taking what's left over." Passion and hate tinged Amahlé's words. Oadira had known oppression, but a sanitary version, safe behind the plantation house's walls and the protection of the dead queen's magic. Amahlé on the other hand had witnessed the pain, rape, and degradation, not from behind glass, but in stark bloody reality. Her scars were not emotional or the result of watching other people suffer. They were the results of her own suffering.

"I'll never forget that," Princess Oadira said.

"The obsidian chains have had damaging effects on the slaves on this estate, making them docile and forcing them to accept their current situation," Amahlé said, now looking through the window as well. "They've been experimenting on the children to see if they use them at an early age, if it affects their disposition to rebel later. I've heard them whisper about eventually not needing the chains at all, because the next generation of slaves will have no will of their own to fight back."

Silence fell on the barn as Princess Oadira and Amahlé opened the large door. As pristine as the outside looked, the inside was the exact opposite, like a sepulcher made from white marble but filled with rotting flesh inside. The wood on the barn's interior was wilted, smelling of mold, feces, and urine with decomposing remains filling the air. The putrid scent increased as Amahlé and Oadira stepped inside. Oadira's eyes blurred at the sight before her. Hundreds of slaves were cuffed in powerful obsidian chains, kneeling in dirty hay. Some of them even had obsidian masks covering their faces, nailed to the base of their skulls so they couldn't be removed. Their skin was stained with dried blood, pupils black and devoid of any consciousness.

"What is this?" Oadira asked, desperately looking to Amahlé for answers. "Why are these masks nailed to their heads?!?"

"They're the slaves resistant to the Madame's obsidian chains," Amahlé answered slowly, eyes engulfed with rage. She touched the head of the closest captive, but he didn't respond. "They're isolated from the others to exterminate all resemblance of hope to the point of stripping them of their mother tongue."

"Why didn't you tell me?" Oadira whispered. Even one of the small boys wore a mask. The marks of the nails in his skull were fresh.

"You knew they did experiments out here," Amahlé said

with a shrug.

Oadira grabbed the older woman by the shoulders and forced her to look the princess in the eye. "I didn't know about this!"

"Because you didn't want to know!" Amahlé shouted back. Veins on her forehead throbbed. Her eyes bulged like a mad woman. "You were chosen to lead us. I've known that from the moment I saw you as a child. But don't pretend you suffered like we've suffered. Don't act shocked by the atrocities of our oppressors. They deserve what they're about to get. They deserve death and pain and fear. Do you doubt this?"

"No," Oadira said without hesitation. Again, the reality of the pain her brothers and sisters had suffered became incredibly real to her. "The day of rebellion is upon us. We will no longer have to endure the sight of our people in chains. I'm sorry I didn't look as closely as I should have. I know and understand your pain."

"We feel it every moment of every passing day," Amahlé said, voice growing quiet.

"My heart aches for what you've all had to go through. We are more than these witan devils portray us as," Oadira said.

Together, the two women began singing the song of freedom. While the chained slaves didn't respond with words, their eyes seemed to come alive. Several blinked and shook their heads as if casting off a nightmare. A few others stood on tired feet and held their chains over their heads.

Even here, in the darkest most tyrannical section of Lalaurie's estate, where hope itself had been strangled in its crib, a light of freedom began to flicker.

Oadira and Amahlé made their way back to the plantation house in time for dinner. Madame Lalaurie asked about Oadira's time with Nezikiah. Oadira talked about his tenderness and how she was certain he had impregnated her with a strong warrior son that would bring honor and riches to the Lalaurie family.

Overseer Plummer drank wine in the corner, eyeing Oadira the entire time. He mumbled something about singing slaves and how a couple lower overseers were whipped for letting it happen.

Oadira felt a twinge of regret that they hadn't been hanged like she initially thought.

They certainly deserved it.

As the sun set, Madame Lalaurie left for her night out gambling. Since paying off her blackmailer (Oadira wondered what the Madame would say if she knew it had been Solomon all along holding the murder of her husband over her head), she had been frequenting the game halls, and doing quite well for herself by all accounts. As soon as her carriage was out of sight, and Plummer confirmed to be relaxing with one of the slave women from the orchards, Oadira and Amahlé snuck out to where they knew the heads of the different slave families would be waiting for them. They arrived at the firepit where marriage ceremonies and equinox prayers were held, though no fire raged tonight to draw attention to the gathering. The sky grew dark overhead as a grove of trees ringed the area, the smell of ash and burned wood still on the warm breeze.

The hundreds of slaves started murmuring among themselves as Oadira stepped forward. They bowed to her, eventually quieting down so she could talk.

Oadira had never addressed a crowd of people before. Over the past several months she had talked to many of the people here tonight personally, but never all at once. What words could she say that would inspire them all to continue with their plan? Many of them would kill at her command tonight. Many of them would die. She had gone from an angry woman in a plantation house ready to run away at the threat of being sold off for her breeding ability, into a princess and revolutionary. Solomon had faith in her. Now she needed to have faith in herself.

"I ask you all to be ready to take the next step in fighting for our freedom," Princess Oadira said as she stood in front of those ready to fight. "The first spirituals have been sung. We act tonight. There will be no going back. You now have maps that will lead you to freedom. The witans operating the breeding farms and the brothels must not be able to leave. During your midnight shift changes, the witans need to be wiped out—all of them. After they are killed, housekeeping will come in and store their bodies in the large laundry bins until they are all dead."

"What about Mr. Plummer and the overseers?" asked one of the members of the crowd.

"The slaves in the main quarters will start with the overseers first, the slave-catching police second, and then the slave owners on the surrounding estates. Has word been sent to the other plantations in the area?"

"It has, princess," one of the older men said, scratching his gray beard. "My sons took the hidden path through the forest this afternoon as soon as the songs had been sung. They returned an hour ago. Everyone is ready."

"Excellent," Oadira continued. "This will lead to the disruption of the nautical slave trade in Lucedale, Vannadale, and Abingdale. I know you feel defeated and broken down. I know you wanted to fight and have had to restrain yourself from doing so. I know you have waited years for when I was ready. That time has now come."

She looked out on her people as they muttered their approval. Some of the men held tools and sticks, anything that could be used as a weapon. Even so, she knew not everyone had answered the call. Some of the Sahaelian slaves had chosen to stay back, either out of fear or the belief they couldn't win.

"There are members of our families and our people who are not here tonight," Oadira said slowly. "They have chosen not to join in our rebellion. They are of our kind. Many of them will fight against us. They will need to be put down but not killed. We need to be wary of the spies among us, the witan dogs, the sell-outs, and skin deceivers."

"Then we kill them!" called a voice from the crowd.

"We do not kill our own," Oadira said, putting her hands up to calm an angry swell that seemed to ripple through the mob.

"All skinfolk ain't kinfolk!" shouted a woman holding a young girl on her hip.

"I have a solution for our fake brothers and sisters," Oadira said. Solomon had been aware of this eventuality and had given her an idea on how to handle Sahaelians who fought for their oppressors. He had spoken with kindness about their betrayal and how ignorance and fear had gotten the better of them. Still, he told her they needed to be dealt with quickly even so. "You are to use chloroform to incapacitate them, so they won't be able to warn Madame Lalaurie. We've taken some from the labs where they embalm the bodies of the witan barons. Amahlé will be passing out jars. Now, all of you here tonight know what our mission is. Your responsibilities are to wipe out the witan slave masters, their men and women, old and young," she looked at Amahlé and focused on all the pain that had been caused over the past 15 years. "…Children and babies—kill them all. We are not here to be forgiving tonight. We cannot care for anyone but our own. Sahael is our destination, and only children of Sahael can make the journey. If we were to leave the young alive, they would suffer and starve with their parents dead. Madame Lalaurie often told me that what she did to all of us was a mercy. Our slaughtering of the witans and their young tonight will be exactly that: a mercy."

A cheer split the night. Men howled and cried as if releasing a decade of pent-up frustration. Hearing Princess Oadira's words and the passion deep within her voice, something within these slaves was unlocked. She became their moral compass; they were ready to give their lives for her at a moment's notice. Princess Oadira and Amahlé had convinced the slaves to lead the rebellion, creating the diversion in Lucedale, allowing her to sneak onto the ships and set out on the next stage of her mission.

After speaking to the crowd, Oadira and Amahlé made their way back to the estate house. The moonless sky looked down on them as they walked silently. There would be blood for blood tonight. Oadira, originally hesitant, now anticipated the carnage, knowing it was the first salvo in a war that would remake the world. In decades to come, peace would reign from Sahael and spread over Aarde, but for now, only death would get them there.

As they approached the dark house, a scream caused the birds in the tree out front to take flight in surprise. Oadira stopped for a second before running up the front stairs and throwing open the door. Mr. Plummer stood in the parlor beating a slave girl with a cowbell. The girl frothed at the mouth and passed out due to extreme pain.

"That's enough!" Princess Oadira yelled.

Plummer jumped in surprise, cheeks quickly turning red as he sneered at Oadira.

"You don't get to talk to me like that, bitch," he drawled, brushing his long greasy hair away from his forehead.

Njiru's rings and Nebiriau's bracelet blazed brighter than ever before. A blue glow seemed to fill the room. All the emotions Oadira had been feeling, from the excitement of the slaves, to her own feelings of inadequacy, bubbled to the surface. Though she had never done so before, a dagger of blue crystal materialized in her hand as if in response to an unspoken command. Her Orishan artes had manifested in a new and unexpected way.

Oadira moved quickly, jumping toward the pudgy cretin, and sliced Mr. Plummer's throat in a single movement. A look of shock spread his eyes wide as he grabbed at his bleeding gullet. He coughed, trying to curse at his enemy, but fell face-first onto the rug. He convulsed a few times, spitting blood onto Oadira's bare feet. After a few more guttural chokes, Plummer's legs kicked and twitched before lying still. The rug turned crimson as a pool of blood spread from his severed throat.

"What have you done?!" Amahlé asked as Oadira swayed from side to side. She dropped the knife as exhaustion seemed to flow through her muscles after using her Orishan artes in a way she never had before.

Everything became a blur of movement. Amahlé called out. Several of the slaves entered and picked Oadira up. Others pulled Plummer's body outside. As the men carried Oadira onto the front porch, she began to sing the final song softly. The slaves started humming the tune. It filled Oadira's ears as if the words echoed from every direction. Even with her eyes closed she knew the slaves were singing the words while walking across Madame Lalaurie's estate, ready to take back their lives.

Follow the drinkin' gourd

Follow the drinkin' gourd

For the old man is comin' just to carry you to freedom

Follow the drinkin' gourd

When the sun comes back, and the first quail calls

Follow the drinkin' gourd

For the old man is waiting just to carry you to freedom

Follow the drinkin' gourd

Follow the drinkin' gourd

Follow the drinkin' gourd

For the old man is waiting to carry you to freedom

Follow the drinkin' gourd

Well, the riverbank makes a mighty good road

Dead trees will show you the way

Left foot, peg foot, travelin' on

Follow the drinkin' gourd

Follow the drinkin' gourd

Follow the drinkin' gourd

For the old man is waiting to carry you to freedom

Follow the drinkin' gourd

Well, the river ends, between two hills

Follow the drinkin' gourd

There's another river on the other side

Follow the drinkin' gourd

Follow the drinkin' gourd

Follow the drinkin' gourd

For the old man is waiting to carry you to freedom

Follow the drinkin' gourd

Well, where the great big river meets the little river

Follow the drinkin' gourd

The old man is waiting to carry you to freedom

Follow the drinkin' gourd

Follow the drinkin' gourd

Follow the drinkin' gourd

For the old man is waiting to carry you to freedom

Follow the drinkin' gourd

For the old man is waiting just to carry you to freedom

If you follow the drinkin' gourd

The song touched the ears of the enslaved, setting them on their path of death and freedom. Soon screams mingled with the words. Oadira tried to stay awake, but fatigue got the best of her. Amahlé breathlessly gave instructions to the men carrying Oadira.

"Get her upstairs!" Oadira could hear Amahlé shouting. "I don't know what's come over her! Keep her safe at all costs!"

Oadira tried to continue listening but fell into a dark realm of dreamless sleep as the cries of slaughtered witans echoed through the plantation.

CHAPTER II
THE COST OF FREEDOM

Lucedale Colony, Lalaurie Estate

Oadira awoke in her room. Bright colors danced outside her window. Was it morning? Had she passed out and slept all night? Conjuring the knife had been more emotional than intellectual. She hadn't consciously made the choice until the blade was already in her hand. Apparently her Orishan Artes had a physical impact beyond what she expected.

Breathing deeply, a smell of ash and smoke filled her nostrils. Muted screams pounded against the windows. Oadira sat up, eyes wide. The colors outside weren't from the sunrise.

The estate was on fire.

The rebellion had started; it was the diversion needed for her to get away from Madame Lalaurie's estate.

Jumping up, Oadira ran toward the door. Smoke seeped up from between the floorboards and jam. She coughed, running back to the window. Fire made its way up the side of the mansion, licking at the shingles.

How had the house caught on fire? Had rebelling slaves set it ablaze without knowing she had passed out inside? What was going on? What had she missed?

Neither climbing out the window or running through a burning building seemed like a good option, but she had to pick one without time to deliberate.

Oadira ran with full force through the door, entering the hallway of the mansion. Heat immediately hit her in the face, along with rising vapors from charred wood. Smoke choked her lungs and she hacked. Oadira quickly tore off her right sleeve and placed the fabric over her mouth. The hallway floor started to weaken as more smoke moved through it. Dropping to her hands and knees, Princess Oadira crawled down the corridor to reach the stairs.

Practically jumping from step to step, Oadira entered the center of the foyer. Flames seared the upholstered couches and chairs, turning a painting of Madame Lalaurie above the mantle into a black mass of carbonized cinders. Fire burned Madame Lalaurie's mansion from the inside.

Just as a beam groaned overhead with the threat of the house's collapse, Oadira darted through the front door into the night. She tripped on something on the porch and turned to see the body of one of the men who had rushed her upstairs as she had been passing out. Blood pooled from a deep gash across his chest. His dead eyes reflected the light from the burning house.

Two more men, both of whom she recognized from her speech earlier that night, lay splayed out on the grass dead. Hundreds of slaves, witans, and guards ran and fought all around in the light of the mansion's conflagration. She watched as the mayhem unfolded before her eyes, seeing her brothers and sisters fight and kill for their freedom at all costs.

"There she is!" a man shouted to her left. Oadira turned to see Overseer Fredric, a tall black man who had betrayed his people and lived only to serve Madame Lalaurie. He was a skin-traitor and selfish rapist. A bloodhound pulled against a leash in his hands and barked at Oadira. "Get 'er!" Fredric screamed.

Without thinking, Oadira turned and ran. She passed several slaves beating an overseer to death with a rock, along with a handful of teenage boys carrying torches and setting fire to bales of hay next to the barns. It must have been them who torched the mansion with Oadira inside.

A growl pulled her attention behind her. The bloodhound had caught up easily. It jumped at Oadira, fangs bared, spit flinging from its tongue.

Much like when she had seen Overseer Plummer attacking the young slave, the bracelet on Oadira's wrist glowed blue and she felt a blade materialize in her palm. With a slash of azure light, Oadira decapitated the bloodhound just as it went to sink its teeth into her neck. The weight of the canine pushed her back. Oadira tripped and fell in the dirt, feeling the warmth of blood on her hands. The dog's body lay motionless beside her.

The stars overhead twirled as if Oadira's world was spinning. Once again, she felt an exhaustion she didn't understand. No matter how tired she was, Oadira knew she had to get up and run. Overseer Frederic, or some other witan enforcer, would find her there and her escape would be thwarted.

"Oadira?" A young voice said. "Princess Oadira?"

Focusing her eyes, Oadira saw the face of one of the teenage boys setting fire to the plantation. Light from his torch accented his dark skin and worried face.

"The overseers are chasing me…" Princess Oadira moaned.

The rebelling youth helped Oadira to her feet.

"I need to get out of here," she said, voice stronger. She still felt unnaturally tired from using the Orishan magics, but her head seemed clearer than it had after killing Plummer.

"I'm coming for ya, ya little niglet," Overseer Fredric said as he turned the corner next to the barn. A look of panic struck his dark face as he saw the dog's body and head separated from each other in front of him. "My hound!" he shrieked. "My hound!"

"Run," one of the boys holding her arms said to Oadira. As she stumbled, the boys rushed Frederic, swinging their torches. She charged around the far corner of the barn toward the road and brothels beyond. A whip cracked behind her, followed by the scream of a teenage boy.

Oadira ran as quickly as she could toward the brothels and the breeding farms. Dead bodies seemed to lie everywhere she looked, some slaves, others witan. At one point she jumped over the corpse of what looked to be a pregnant slave woman whose chest had been slashed with a sword.

Passing the brothels along the road just as she had earlier that afternoon, Oadira now watched as they burned brightly. Witan men who had waited in line to be pleasured now fled naked as their former victims killed them one by one.

Pausing to catch her breath, Oadira coughed again, spitting out smoke particles that had stuck to her throat and lungs from when she escaped the mansion fire. Fumes from burning buildings and trees choked the air with a suffocating oppression. Oadira filled her lungs, but continued coughing, nonetheless.

"I'm coming for you, you murderous bitch!" Overseer Frederic said as he ran through the trees less than a hundred yards away. "You killed my father, Mr. Plummer! No kids with torches gonna stop me!"

Despite her overwhelming fatigue, Oadira ran to the laboratories. As she approached the finely painted barn, an explosion blew the front doors off, spitting fire and debris in all directions. Witan scientists hung from the tree beside the road, nooses made from bedsheets around their necks. They swayed there like laundry in a breeze, not more powerful than dandelion fluff on a spring afternoon. No more powerful than Frederic the bastard overseer.

"I'm done running from weak-minded half-witan men," Princess Oadira spat. She turned from the fire roaring at the laboratory entrance and waited.

Within moments, Overseer Frederic appeared with his nine-foot-long obsidian whip, made from the toughest kind of cowhide and loaded with lead. It had been known to take the skin off an ox. It was not an uncommon thing to see the new slaves with their backs mangled in the most horrible way.

"I'm going to whip you to the organs, cut you up, and throw you to the pigs to be erased from the witan world," Overseer Frederic said as he sauntered toward Oadira.

He swung his whip toward her head.

Oadira dodged the attack, pivoting to the left and grabbing Overseer Frederic's whip with her right hand. She pulled on the cord, forcing Frederick to stumble to the ground. Jumping forward, Oadira kicked the man in his face. He cried out and fell onto his back.

"It ends here tonight for you," Oadira said as she placed her foot on Frederic's neck. He punched at her legs, clawing at her dress, spitting curses that couldn't leave his throat. As he stopped struggling and gasped for breath, she grabbed his whip, wrapping it around his neck before hurling one end over a branch next to the scientists hanging in the tree. With a forceful tug, Oadira lifted Frederic off his feet and left him dangling until his legs stopped kicking.

Oadira shifted her sight to the burning cotton fields filled with hordes of her people rising up and fighting for their freedom, killing witans wherever they could.

Fire lifted from the innocent livestock running frantically across the estate. Open rebellion broke out on Madame Lalaurie's plantation. The slaves, inspired by Oadira's courage and inner strength, removed the magical obsidian chains, and set them ablaze. Oadira joined in the destruction. Like a drunk woman inflamed by liquor, she grabbed a lit torch from the ground and set fire to a bundle of hay next to a barn full of cattle. It caught fire and burned brightly, attracting the attention of everyone on the plantation. Screams caught her attention, and she ran toward them, finding estate overseers beating a group of children no older than 10 or 11 years old. Plummer had died by her hand tonight. His bastard son Frederic had died too. These men deserved no better fate.

She then crept up on them from behind, slicing their throats from ear to ear with a conjured sapphire dagger, freeing the rebelling slaves they had corralled and captured. Each time she manifested a weapon it became easier and less tiring. She knew that once the adrenaline stopped pumping in her veins she would likely collapse, but for now, nothing could stop her from seeking revenge and retribution against her oppressors.

Slave catchers, bloodhounds, and police were everywhere as Oadira ran through the cornfields trying to find a safe path to the ships just as she and Solomon had planned. The river inlet leading to the sea was only a few miles away, but the commotion at the plantation seemed to have attracted every witan man in the area.

Oadira quickly ran to the eastern side of the plantation. She knew she needed to make it there before the colonial militia showed up, ruining her chances of getting out of Lucedale for good.

After another mile of running, Oadira's lungs burned, and her legs threatened to give out. She stumbled from one of the wheatfields onto a dirt road not far from the river docks. She could still smell the smoke from the plantation fires, but the air tasted fresher out here, kissed by a slight breeze. Up ahead she saw torches on the road as a group of people gathered and shouted. Creeping closer just inside the stalks of wheat, Oadira saw a makeshift checkpoint had been set up. A group of seven overseers with bloodhounds, along with four men on horseback, listened to orders being barked from a short older woman in a frilly white dress with blue accents and graying curled hair.

Madame Lalaurie.

She must have returned early from her night of gambling. Solomon had hoped her absence would have led to more confusion among her underlings, but apparently that would not be the case at this point.

Oadira had to get past the inspection checkpoint to get off the estate. This was the fastest route to the ships. If she had to backtrack, it would force her to travel halfway back across the estate, with the bloodhounds and the slave-catching police closing in on her.

What could she do? Even with her new-found abilities to conjure weapons, she couldn't beat this many people.

Her heart began to pound faster, even though she was no longer running. It seemed like her escape would be thwarted. What would that mean for the hundreds of slaves fighting and dying right now? Oadira was their hope for a brighter future. Her capture would mean the end of their faith in freedom. Another generation or more might remain enslaved if tonight failed.

She couldn't let that happen.

But what could she do?

Sweat dripped from her nose as she began to cry softly. One of the dogs barked in her direction, causing Oadira to jump.

"Hey!" one of the overseers shouted. "The dogs done smell

something. Maybe somebody done hid in the wheat. Check it!"

No! It couldn't end this way!

Just as Oadira turned to run, her tattoos lit up all over her body Nebiriau's bracelet and Njiru's rings lit up as well. An intense pain radiated in every muscle in her body. Oadira's teeth clenched, and she fell to the dirt as she hear bloodhounds sniffing nearby. Her whole body burned from the inside out as she tried to hold back her screams, trying not to give away her position as she moaned. For a moment, Oadira thought she would die from the pain. It was as if someone were peeling the skin from her body and reattaching it inside out.

"What the hell you doing lyin' out here boy?" A man's voice said as a boot tapped her leg. "Get up! We done thought you was a slave hiddin' out here."

Oadira opened her eyes as a wet dog tongue licked her cheek. She rose to her feet, noticing the skin on her hands had changed. It no longer looked dark brown as it had her entire life. It was pale pink and new. Her jaw hurt, as did her shoulders.

A realization dawned. Solomon had mentioned she would eventually be able to change how she looked. Her body had morphed into that of a slave catcher. She was now disguised as the people charged with searching for her with pale witan skin and a tan outfit.

"What you doin' out here, boy?" the overseen asked as he grabbed Oadira under the arm to help her stand. "No slaves done attacked you, did they?"

"No, I just got lost and fell," Oadira answered, voice shockingly deep in her ears.

"What's going on?" Madame Lalaurie asked as Oadira stumbled from the wheat with the old overseer.

"Just one of the kids getting lost in all the crazy," the

overseer said. He patted Oadira on the back. “Get goin’, son. Head back to the homesteads.”

“Yes sir,” she said.

Oadira walked through the group of men with their swords, torches, and pitchforks. Several of them nodded at her as she passed, others pointed and shouted about burning some of the nigger slaves to death in front of their families to teach them all a lesson.

“Find Oadira!” Madame Lalaurie shouted as Oadira walked briskly away from the checkpoint. “She’s worth more than all these damn slaves combined!”

Turning a corner in the road, the lights from the torches disappeared. Oadira started to run again, but only made it a few yards when her body started to burn from the inside out. Once again, she doubled over on the road, gagging and coughing. It was as if every vein in her body was twisting and contorting all at once. Quickly, she shifted back into her natural form. Covered in sweat, Oadira tumbled into the small ditch next to the grain fields. She gasped for air, mind calling out for anyone to help her. She couldn’t move, couldn’t think, couldn’t speak.

Amahlé, her mind called. Where was Amahlé? Had she survived all of this? Was she dead somewhere at that very moment?

Oadira had no idea how long she lay there. It could have been hours or days as far as she was concerned. A voice brought her back to her senses. A voice she recognized.

“Oadira!”

It was Amahlé’s voice.

“Oadira!” Amahlé said again. “Get up, child. You need to get up!”

"How did you…find me?" Oadira asked, words little more than a whisper.

"You called out to me with your Orishan abilities. I heard you. I felt your pull and knew where to come. You need to get up, child."

Oadira stood, leaning on Amahlé for support. Her educator had heard her cries for help and came running. She was alive. Oadira wanted to weep with joy but couldn't find the strength to shed tears.

"We need to get you to the ships," Amahlé continued, guiding Oadira along the dark road. "Madame Lalaurie has set up checkpoints everywhere. So many of the witans are dead, but the entire region seems to have arrived to help her crush the rebellion. Many slaves have died, but many have escaped. It's time you joined them. That witan woman is driven by her hatred to find you. She considers you her property. What's worse? She sees you as less than a person and her most prized possession that has brought her so much wealth and standing."

"That witan sees me as three-fifths of a person," Oadira replied. Each step was difficult, but her strength seemed to be returning, along with her resolve. "I now understand what Solomon meant about White Darkness permeating the hearts of all witans in Aarde."

They walked for another two hours. Slowly, the sky to the east began to grow light. Several times during their journey they had to hide along the road as horses ran past or a carriage rumbled along at dangerous speeds. Eventually they could smell water in the air. They were drawing close. Masts took shape above them in the growing dawn. The sound of chains rattling and sailors chattering mingled with gulls flapping and calling overhead.

Amahlé and Oadira stepped out of the fading darkness into a crowd of people approaching the ships. Merchants called out for cargo manifests while bosuns loaded crates of fruit preserves onto loading crates.

Oadira kept her head down. All she needed to do was get to the boat leaving for Iceoth at Dock 7. That was the plan. Everything would be alright once she made it to that ship.

"There she is! Get that Nigger," yelled Madame Lalaurie suddenly. Oadira turned to see her matron standing on a platform across the docks, finger pointed in her direction. "When I get my hands on you, I am going to skin you alive and feed you to cannibals."

Without plan or thought, Oadira and Amahlé pushed through the crowd, knocking over several surprised sailors. They needed to make it to Dock 7. Run toward Dock 7. Boots thumped against wood not far behind them. The pursuit would be unending now that they knew Oadira meant to sail away forever.

"We're not going to make it. They're closing in on us," Oadira said, panting heavily.

"It's me," Educator Amahlé said as she made eye contact with Oadira, signaling goodbye in her eyes. "I'm slowing you down." Amahlé let go of Oadira's hand and darted toward Dock 5 and a ship pulling up the gangplank in preparation to set sail.

"What are you doing?" Oadira yelled, grabbing Amahlé's hand before she could run off.

"I need to draw them away to give you more time to get to the ships," Amahlé said. "I promise you they'll not catch me."

"No, let's leave together," Oadira said.

"No!" Amahlé yelled, pulling away. "This is the only way to secure your freedom." Amahlé caressed Oadira's face and kissed her on the forehead. She bolted in the opposite direction, drawing attention toward the departing ship. Oadira turned and ran, tears in her eyes.

Within moments, Oadira reached the ship leaving for Iceoth. Slaves stood in a staggered line, waiting for orders from their captors. Oadira joined the line, blending in as best she could.

This won't work, she thought frantically. *Lalaurie is going to search the lines. I might as well shout to her where I am.*

The line moved forward at the shout of the captain and the slaves lumbered toward the ship. As the line marched, the slaves stepped over the lifeless body of an old woman who had died at some time in the night. Her lifeless eyes stared unblinking toward the brightening sky above.

Oadira knew this was her opportunity.

She quickly took on the form of the dead, aged woman as the encrusted magic from Njiru's rings protected her. She knew she could do it since she had already a few hours before. This time though, instead of her subconscious picking a witan boy as her new vessel, Oadira consciously chose the woman lying dead before her. Her muscles burned again, but the transformation was less extreme and thus less painful. Her skin sagged, back stooping, and before anyone noticed, Oadira had been replaced with an aged woman sorrowful and dying.

"Check them all!" Madame Lalaurie shouted. "Check every goddamn one!"

The Madame and her men inspected each broken down and dying slave being loaded onto the ships. After an initial sweep, Lalaurie had them searched again, and then a third time.

Finally, with the slaves loaded onto the ships, they were inspected a fourth time by Madame Lalaurie personally to make sure Oadira had not gotten on any of the boats. The line moved as Oadira shuffled to the front, presenting herself as a broken-down, dying slave with frail bones, missing yellow teeth, and whitish-gray hair.

She stared into Madame Lalaurie's frantic eyes, bloodshot and tired. The woman grabbed Oadira's cheeks and shifted her head back and forth to make sure she wasn't missing anything. After inspecting her thoroughly, the Madame allowed her to go with the other slaves.

Before Lalaurie left the ship, she glanced back over her shoulder. The look in her eyes was one of desperation and defeat. She had lost her prize possession tonight, along with her house, likely all of her witan overseers, and a massive proportion of her slave labor force. Oadira felt no pity for her, wishing instead that she could watch over the coming days as the woman learned that her other two princesses were gone as well. Solomon would make sure of it. Lalaurie was about to lose everything, and it couldn't have happened to a nicer woman.

Soon the ship set sail for Iceoth. Oadira hobbled along the deck seeing cages with kids in them, not unlike what she had experienced 15 years before after the fall of Sahael. Flashbacks came painfully to her mind.

On the captain's orders, she followed the weak and dying slaves down to their quarters at the bottom of the ship.

Once she settled in, an enormous sigh of relief blew out of her mouth, putting her at ease. The boat rocked slowly, evidence of the fact they had left the docks and were now being pulled toward the open sea. Lalaurie could do nothing to stop them now.

Huddled in a dark corner, Oadira realized she was alone. She morphed back into her standard form. Sitting there for a while, Oadira thought about what had happened over the last 24 hours. She saw Solomon for what could very well be the last time. The fire in the plantation house had burned the maps and instructions Solomon had left behind to help her on her journey. She had used her abilities effectively, conjuring sapphire blades and even changing her appearance. She had inspired the slaves to act and be free. She had killed Plummer, Frederic, and other overseers. Their deaths did not bother her. And beyond all of that, Amahlé had heard her thoughts and come to her aid. Could she communicate with others telepathically beyond her cousins, or was her bond with Educator Amahlé special?

The longer Oadira sat alone in the corner, the more tired she became, but her mind continued racing.

The maps and instructions Solomon had left to help on her journey had been destroyed in the fire. She had no way of knowing where to go. He told her his instructions would make sense once she arrived in Iceoth, but she no longer had them as a reference. She had read through them once a month or so ago but hadn't memorized them since she knew she wouldn't need them until later. Now they were ash and couldn't help her.

What would she do?

Closing her eyes, Oadira allowed herself to rest and sleep. Even in the uncomfortable ship's hold, her fatigue got the better of her. By the time she awoke, she had no idea how long she had slept, but she felt strong once again, as if being free from the Lalaurie estate had reinvigorated her spirit.

To her surprise, a young man now sat across from her, looking at her with a peaceful expression on his face.

One of Njiru's rings illuminated with a blue light. The young man noticed it, as did Oadira, who felt shocked that the pale azure light now drew unwanted attention to her. She remained calm, staring at the young man nervously. He was handsome, with long, dreadlocked hair and a firm jaw. Unlike the other slaves who were emaciated and frail, this man appeared robust and strong, as if he could work all day long and not have it bother him at all. His seven-foot frame was kingly; his teeth white as ivory.

"I saw what you did to get here," he whispered in a deep

soothing voice. “It was very impressive. I saw as you ran toward the ship. It was obvious you were being hunted by the witans. I watched as you took the form of that old woman who died. You’re not the only one who has used the artes of our people to enter this ship.” The young man leaned over and whispered even quieter, “The Signs are upon us.”

He smiled and nodded to Oadira, as if waiting for her to give a specific response. She stared at him in confusion. Oadira did not know what he was waiting for her to do. She remembered Solomon speaking those same words, but he never gave her any instructions regarding them. The young man stared, waiting for some unknown reaction.

“What’s your name?” Oadira asked as the silence grew more uncomfortable.

“Ozias Ocnus. And yours?”

“Oadira,” she answered quickly. “Why are you on this ship, Ozias Ocnus?”

“I had to sneak onto this ship to get back home,” Ozias said.

“Home? Why?” Oadira asked.

“Iceoth is my ancestral home. It is where my people have lived for over four hundred years. We have succeeded by remaining in isolation.”

“Sahaelians?”

“Yes.”

“No one knows where your people are?” Oadira asked softly.

“No one knows anything about our presence, and my people plan on keeping it that way,” said Ozias.

Oadira contemplated his words. Her mind swam with

questions. Had he been a slave too? How did he know about Iceoth? Was he born there? Too many queries to voice, especially as Oadira looked into his handsome face, feeling the confidence his natural presence seemed to radiate.

"How is that possible?" she asked. "The witans know all about the people of Sahael and where we fled. Natas is known to have hunted us without rest. I've met him face-to-face. Strength and wickedness drip off of him. The stories are true, I know it. How have your people remained hidden?"

Ozias stared questioningly at Oadira. He seemed surprised by her line of questioning. "I think it's about time we get some rest. You couldn't have been comfortable sleeping against the hull as you have been for the past hour."

"Why are you not answering my question?" Oadira asked.

"We are many days away from the Iceoth coast, and we are in a good hiding spot. I have enough extra rations for three people," he mentioned to Oadira, implying he would share with her.

"What happens if we run out?" asked Oadira.

"If we should run out, the others on this ship will make sure we are fed and taken care of," Ozias said.

"Why are these people taking care of you?" Oadira inquired.

"Why do you care?" Ozias seemed to be growing increasingly suspicious of Oadira's questions.

"They have to eat too!" Oadira said.

"They will. Do not worry about it," Ozias said.

"How?" Oadira asked, suddenly feeling warm and clammy. "I'm tired of people telling me things will be alright. Are you as bad as the witans? Taking from those weaker than you and pretending it's for their own good?"

Ozias seemed to bristle at her words, back going straight as he kneeled in front of her. "You talk too much. Shut up! I would like to get some sleep."

"Do not tell me to shut up!" Oadira shouted.

Ozias chuckled dryly. "Why?"

"Because I said so!" Oadira said. Once again, a pale blue light filled the space, but it wasn't from Oadira's bracelet or rings; it was from her angry eyes.

Ozias raised his eyebrow and smiled. "Hey?"

"What?" Oadira said, frowning.

"Shut up!" Ozias laughed out loud. He seemed suddenly playful, not harsh or mean.

Oadira didn't necessarily appreciate the levity. "I said, don't tell me to shut up!"

"What? Are you going to glow your eyes at me?"

"I can do more than that," Oadira threatened, though his smile made her less inclined to form a knife and cut his face.

"I just did it again!" Ozias doubled over in laughter.

"Why is this so funny?"

Ozias stopped laughing and shifted his legs, so he leaned against the hull. "You really don't understand the culture of our people, do you?"

"Not if our culture is about disrespect."

"So, you didn't like it when I told you to shut up?"

"No! Why would I?"

"How about, 'Stop talking' then?"

"I will not stop talking until you tell me more about

yourself," Oadira said.

Ozias straightened his posture and furrowed his eyebrows. "Alright, what do you want to know?"

"Are your people really from Sahael?"

"Yes. In the times before."

"Before what? Natas' invasion?"

Ozias scratched his armpit. "Long before that, but the invasion changed things for some of us."

"Like what?"

"You talk too much."

Oadira's hands began to shake. Solomon had told her to go to Iceoth, a barren place with very few people. If what Ozias was telling her, a remnant of Sahael still lived in that frozen land.

"When we get to the shores, can you take me with you?" Oadira's face was dead serious.

"Hell no!" Ozias said with a deep frown.

"Why not?" Oadira asked.

Ozias scoffed. "You seem like a lot of trouble, more than I can handle. I mean, you are beautiful, but I'm guessing that comes with a price. So, no."

"But you could be a big help!" Oadira said.

"I never disappoint." His prideful smile was back. "Let us get some sleep now."

"No! my rings glowed when I saw you. That means something."

"And your eyes glowed when you got mad at me. For all I know you're a witch of some kind who murders little children."

Again, the man smirked playfully.

"Will you at least think about it?" Oadira pleaded. She felt strange begging a young man she did not know for help finding a people she knew nothing about, but Solomon wanted her to go to Iceoth for a reason, and the rings had glowed when she noticed this man. That meant something. She needed him. Oadira felt their fates were intertwined; she just didn't know how, but she had a feeling that she needed to keep this person in her life.

"No!" said Ozias. "Listen, you look like you come with a lot of baggage. I don't want to carry those bags."

Oadira stared him directly in the face, locking her eyes with his. "Do you have any respect for a queen?"

Ozias scoffed and nearly choked. "Who?" he asked in between coughs.

"Me!" Oadira said.

"You're a queen? Here, in a slave ship? Look, I saw what you did when you got on the boat, and I thought maybe you had something of worth to offer, but if you expect me to believe you're a queen, you better have something better than glowing rings and skin changing abilities. I've seen all that before. Now go to sleep."

Oadira shrugged her shoulders. "Fine! But I'll just start this all over again in the morning."

Ozias rolled his eyes and shook his head. "Okay," he said before he turned and settled into his hiding spot.

When morning came, Oadira had no desire to talk any further with this cocky Ozias. He seemed more like Madame Lalaurie's overseers than he did a Sahaelian from a proud lost people. He was a con artist, nothing more. Handsome, but disposable, because he saw everyone around him as being disposable.

She would continue her journey to Iceoth as Solomon had instructed. She would follow her gut and discover what she needed herself without some smug man treating her like she was less than him. At sunrise she went up on deck, took the form of the old woman once again, and began making and preparing food for all the rejected Alkebulan people who were hungry.

Ozias eventually came up from below deck. He looked at Oadira for a while as if trying to solve a puzzle. After a few minutes, he jumped in and helped serve the people as well.

Each morning Oadira did the same thing, changed her shape, gathered what food had been left for the slaves, and started helping those stricken with sickness and hunger. Ozias would soon join her, never saying a word.

After four days, Oadira realized she had grown comfortable with their silence, and was more than happy for it to continue. But, like a moment of peace after a storm, the quiet couldn't last forever.

"What brings you to this ship?" Ozias finally asked on the afternoon of the fourth day. Oadira was in the form of the old woman, leaning over the ship side looking at the ocean.

"I just needed to get out of Lucedale for reasons that are my own," Oadira answered.

"So, you would just leave, not knowing where you were going?" Ozias asked.

Oadira thought to herself for a moment and pondered on Ozias's question. Ozias was right. Sure, she was following Solomon's instructions to go to Iceoth and eventually make her way to Alkebulan and the capital of Sahael, but other than that, she had no idea what she was supposed to do or where she was supposed to go. She had just left Lucedale, not knowing anything beyond the need to head to the outer lands.

"I don't have anywhere to go, truly; it just seemed now was the perfect time to escape," Oadira said. "I've been branded a runaway slave and soon will be diagnosed by the witan doctors with drapetomania."

"What's that?" Ozias asked.

"A condition for wanting to be free. The Madame will send the police and slave catchers after me and will not stop until I'm caught or killed. If the doctors believe I have drapetomania they'll simply sell me to someone else. At least looking like the old woman when I'm in their presence, they won't pay too much attention to me." She looked at her wrinkled hands. "I wonder what her name was."

Ozias spat into the ocean. "Drapetomania. Our people truly suffer. I didn't understand it before I arrived here. Even so, the spirit of rebellion has awakened, inserting rebellion in the hearts of all slaves, starting in the colonies of Lucedale, Vannadale, and Abingdale. I was only able to get on this ship because the rebellions hadn't reached my side of Lucedale yet."

Oadira's eyes narrowed. "The rebellions happening all over the colonies aren't a coincidence. I knew this already. How did you know about it?"

"The rebellions are why I've failed to complete the task given to me; they were the perfect distraction," Ozias said. "The signs of rebellion are the prelude to the Sign of the Times. Four hundred years of household, patriarchal, and domestic slavery are ending. Through the spirit of affliction, the four hundred years' prophecy is taking place in the hearts of all Sahaelians, Egyptians, Hornans, and Alkebulans in Aarde. There will be more rebellions that will spread across the world, inspired by other rebellions the

Diaspora are awakening."

"I've heard that phrase before, 'The Signs of the Times,' when I was in Aban City," said Oadira. After a pause to think about what Ozias had said, she asked, "How did you fail?"

"It doesn't matter; we just need to get to Iceoth as soon as possible," Ozias said. "I've said too much for now. Except for that I'm sorry if you felt disrespected the day we met. It was not my intention, though I understand why you took my words that way. I sometimes speak…without thinking."

Oadira smiled and nodded before walking off toward a group of children in their cages asking for water.

The days passed, and Oadira and Ozias continued serving the rejected slaves and learning more about each other. Oadira opened up about her life on the plantation and a bit about what happened the night of her escape. Ozias for his part still spoke in riddles, telling very little about himself. During this time, Oadira had all but mastered the ability to shape-shift back into people and then into her original form each night. At one point she chose a member of the crew so she could sneak extra food to the slaves. While more painful than becoming the old woman, it was far easier than it had been on her first attempt and allowed her to move freely around the ship.

Ozias watched her that night as she transformed back into her natural flesh and settled into their hidden sleeping quarters.

"The people on this ship seem to respect you. Who are you?" he asked.

"No one," Oadira said. "Just an escaped slave like I told you. Maybe I'm a witch that eats children, like you said the night we met."

Ozias bit the side of his bottom lip. He let out a deep exhale and said, "You also told me you were a queen. I thought your tricks were just that: tricks. The longer we're together, the more I doubt that conclusion, and regret how I spoke to you."

"You should have regretted it the moment the words left your lips, no matter who I was," Oadira chided.

"You're right, and I'm sorry. Okay, I will take you with me when we get to the shores of Iceoth, if you still want to meet my people."

"Thanks," Oadira said. Her tone was confident and authoritative, but not excited. "Aren't you worried about carrying my baggage?"

"Some things are worth carrying, I guess," Ozias smiled.

"When will we reach Iceoth?" Oadira asked.

"The temperatures have been dropping for days. This afternoon it started to snow, so I'd bet we'll see the shores tomorrow morning; we need to get our rest."

"If you say so," she said in a cheerful voice. She smiled sweetly and closed her eyes, knowing Ozias was watching her. He wasn't such a bad guy after all, at least not after being humbled a bit.

As day broke, shouts from the upper deck roused Oadira and Ozias. They ran up so quickly Oadira didn't even change her shape. The white frosted shores of Iceoth loomed in front of them, along with the cold air of perpetual winter. Snowflakes fell all around them. Dalean soldiers from sovereign Dales, a witan nation aligned with the Narsan from Western Aarde, stood on the shore in their thick animal hide coats, shooting arrows at slaves jumping ship. Each slave attempting to swim toward the shore would be hit by a volley of arrows, screaming as the ocean turned red. Several sailors across the deck were fighting with a group of slaves, blood covering the wooden hull. Children wrapped in blankets darted across the deck, bare feet slipping on ice that had formed overnight.

"What's going on?" Oadira asked as one of the slave women ran forward and started to climb over the railing.

"The people on this ship are jumping off early, and we need to do the same," the woman said. "The ship has anchored. A few minutes ago, a representative of the Dales came onboard with orders from the Lalaurie estates that arrived here yesterday, to kill every slave! We're all jumping overboard but the Dales are shooting everyone in the water!"

"That witan bitch is hard to evade. Why is all of this happening?" Oadira asked.

"Watch out!" a man shouted. Three slaves grabbed one of the sailors and threw him into the ocean while one of his compatriots stabbed a slave in the back.

Ozias grabbed Oadira's hand as the slave woman leaped from the ship. "When a rebellion starts, they kill all of those who know about it, in order to not to give life to another rebellion. So, they plan to kill every slave man, woman, or child associated with the Madame's estates. Follow my lead. I've learned from previous slaves that have made it safely to these shores. I know how to get us there."

Oadira nodded. Instead of jumping with the frantic slaves, Ozias led Oadira to the far end of the ship, avoiding a fight between a group of sailors and slaves that seemed to be turning to the slave's advantage. They reached the railing and looked down on the cold waters of Iceoth.

"Ready?" he asked.

Air tugged at Oadira's hair as she leaped from the ship. Icy water bit into her flesh as they sank beneath the waves. More than the physical assault however, Oadira suddenly felt a mental attack. Images filled her mind as if in response to the very water that surrounded her.

She saw her younger self, cousins Aamira, and Heziara struggling to tread water as they held on to sea otters pulling them forward. She heard guards shouting and running about with impaired vision thanks to a thick fog resting on the waters. She heard a soft voice in her head, ensuring she would be okay and that she would survive.

She turned her tiny head and saw the beautiful woman kicking the water with her feet. Tears streaked down the woman's face while a soft, angelic smile comforted Oadira. The cold water made her tiny body shiver, but the quiet, reassuring voice calmed her. Suddenly, she could feel herself being carried by a giant bird away from the water and the woman. Tears rolled down her face as the smiling woman disappeared into the distance.

"Hey! Hey!" shouted Ozias. He shook Oadira. "You're in a trance! We need to swim, Oadira!"

Oadira opened her eyes and breathed. She clutched Ozias's hand. He held her tightly, obviously having pulled her to the surface when the vision had hit.

"Swim!" Ozias shouted again. "Follow me!"

"We have stowaways jumping the ship over here! Fire!" said a Dalean guard on shore to their right.

"Dive!" Ozias cried.

On command, the guards fired their arrows. Ozias and Oadira dove to avoid the barrage of arrows, but as they resurfaced, the barrage continued. Bodies floated all around, stuck with arrows like porcupines. Oadira ducked behind one of the corpses just as an arrow swished by her head.

Despite their maneuvers, one arrow struck Oadira on her shoulder blade. She screamed and fell deep into the bloody water. Ozias, who was several breaststrokes ahead, turned and swam back to her.

Pain shot through Oadira's back and chest. She tried to reach the surface but floundered. Ozias' strong hands grabbed her wrist and yanked her up. The water seemed to swirl around Oadira in response to her panic. A brilliant glow emanated from Nebiriau's bracelet. Njiru's rings and Oadira's sapphire eyes illuminated against the early morning light. Suddenly a wave rumbled up behind her and Ozias, pushing them both toward shore. They rolled on the white sand a half mile from the Dalean soldiers.

The sea suddenly seemed to rage like an angry toddler. What moments before had been tranquil ocean, now roiled and frothed with whitecaps. With an unnatural rumble, the water currents pushed the ship away from Iceoth's coast. The Dalean soldier on the shore shouted and cried as another wave rushed inland and smashed them into the rocks of the cliffs to their backs.

Oadira watched, feeling the power of the waves and the swirling eddies beneath the surface.

She had done this.

Much like the first time she had manifested a blade to protect a slave from Mr. Plummer, or her first transformation back in the wheat field weeks before, Oadira had just learned another devastating ability. The waters would answer her call; they would be her hands and feet. They would be her sword.

Her clothes dripped with seawater as her shimmering cerulean eyes resonated with power and authority.

The turbulent ocean waves continued to push the ships away, preventing the guards from shooting the released refugees. Thick layers of fog settled, limiting the vision of the remaining Dalean archers and soldiers.

A look of shock covered Ozias' wet face.

"I knew it," he whispered, eyes locked on the ship as it

tilted and rocked in the waves. "I knew it!" he shouted. "I always fall for the complicated ones! Who are you!?"

Oadira tried to answer, but the pain in her back suddenly consumed her thoughts. She fell forward onto her hands, seeing her reflection in the waters rushing over her fingers.

Her eyes were now bright blue as they had been when they glowed. Only now, they remained blue with an inner light that could no longer be hidden. Her hair also had become a brighter shade than it ever had before. If Natas saw her at this moment, there would be no question of her royalty.

She remembered Solomon's words from their first encounter after the Royal Rumble. He had said, *'The true color of your eyes are hidden now, except when your powers begin to manifest, but soon enough they will return to their true shades permanently. When that time arrives, you will usher in the changing of the times.'*

"Oadira!" Ozias said, rushing to her side. "We need to tend to this wound. And you're freezing! You're not used to the environment like I am."

He knelt and met Oadira at eye level, placing his right hand on her shoulder and turning her to the side, removing the arrow from Oadira's shoulder blade as quickly as he could. Instantly, the pain in her chest subsided. Her breathing returned to normal.

"By the gods," Ozias gasped.

"What is it?" Oadira asked, teeth chattering.

"The wound…it's healing itself. How is this possible? Who are you?"

Oadira leaned against Ozias' chest for warmth and coughed. "I am what I told you I was. I am the last of the Orishan bloodline sent to usher in the changing of the times. I am the High Queen of Sahael. Will you help me?"

"Yes," Ozias said without hesitation.

"Thank you," Oadira replied, closing her eyes.

CHAPTER III

ICEOTH

Iceoth, Benin City, Aarde

Oadira and Ozias stood on an icy, white coast. The pale sand on the shore was frozen over, and for as far as the eye could see, snow flurries drifted from a pale sky. The fierce, bluish-gray waters and currents that pushed the ships away from the shore crashed against one another. Wounded Alkebulans swam and climbed up the frozen Iceoth shore. Oadira could smell their blood in the water, giving off the scent of iron.

"We need to hurry. We do not have much time," Ozias warned.

"We need to help these people get to the beach!" Oadira said.

"No! we're heading to the city," Ozias urged.

Trudging through the cold water, Oadira lifted a weak and injured Alkebulan man to his feet and struggled as she helped him up the shore.

"We don't have enough time!" Ozias insisted.

"These are our people," she exclaimed.

"Ugh! Fine!" said Ozias as he clenched his fists, bringing them down to his side in frustration. Ozias helped Oadira carry the injured Alkebulan man and then helped pull everyone up onto the ice island. After several hours, Ozias and Oadira had successfully helped all the Alkebulan refugees to the white, icy shores of Iceoth. As they both made their way back onto the beach, Oadira looked and gazed over the land for the first time.

Inches of snow covered the ground. Clusters of ice crystals battered the skies and perpetually blanketed the grass. Gelid, blue rivers streamed across the wintry island, as frosted vegetation coated the soil.

"What do we do now?" asked Oadira. "These people will freeze out here." She still felt cold, but an inner heat had warmed her since Ozias had pulled the arrow from her back.

"They're in rags," Ozias replied. "They're barefoot and weak. You and I may not be dressed for the weather, but we're strong. We can make it." He pointed at several slaves shivering, huddled together for warmth with only a few wet blankets wrapped around their shoulders. "There's no way these people are going to make it with the provisions from the ship."

"What provisions?" Oadira yelled. "They were going to kill all of them, and us, on Lalaurie's orders."

"And that death would have been swifter and less painful than what they're about to face," Ozias said, brushing snow from his eyelashes.

As snow fell from the clouds, Oadira scanned the countless Alkebulans who were weary from their struggle and tried nursing their wounds as they lay helpless on the island coast. Without refuge, most, if not all of the slaves wouldn't survive overnight. Their ebony skin and Sahaelian body chemistry naturally made the cold less of a danger than it would for witans, but many were old, wounded, and needed assistance.

"These people need shelter," Oadira said. "Can they follow us?"

"Seriously?" Ozias asked incredulously as he rolled his eyes.

"Yes, I am!" Oadira replied with authority in her voice.

Ozias threw his hands up in the air, giving in to her demands. "Okay. Let's gather them and prepare to have them follow us inland."

Oadira quickly rounded up all the Alkebulans and Sahaelian refugees and ordered them to follow her and Ozias. She tore off the bottom of her dress and wrapped it around her head and neck for protection from the cold.

"This will add hours to our travel," Ozias said as they started walking up a path leading up a cleft between the cliffs. "Some of them won't make it because their wounds are too bad to care for at the moment. We'll make better time on our own, and it will be safer for us just to go without them. We might as well just stay here and die with them."

"I'll die with them if I have to," Oadira spat. "But it won't be huddled together on a snowy shore waiting for death to come."

Hours passed as they slowly headed deeper into the island. Wind blew cold in their faces, with occasional snow flurries turning Oadira's blue hair white. She walked beside Ozias, looking back occasionally to make sure the refugees weren't lagging too far behind. Ozias looked back as well, noticing that some of the refugees were struggling to keep up.

"Not all of these people are going to make it," he said. "We can't stop to help anyone that falls behind."

"That isn't the proper way to treat people. If anyone dies on our journey, then we'll bury them," Oadira answered.

"You don't know this land. I do. Trust me when I tell you, mercy for one will be a death sentence for everyone else."

As Ozias and Oadira traveled farther along a flat plain, one of the refugees fell to his knees too weak to continue as the breath of life and spirit departed his body. Oadira held the refugee man's hand as he died. The man made eye contact with her and smiled before leaving Aarde.

"We need to bury him," Oadira suggested.

"Nonsense," Ozias said.

"Why is that?" asked Oadira with a confused look on her face.

"I told you before; to show mercy to one is to put all the rest in danger. When the body is no longer a living vessel, the soul splits in two, the spirit of life and the spirit that activates the heart. Once they are gone, they leave an empty, unoccupied tabernacle of clay. If you listen just after death takes place, the body begins to sing its symphony."

Oadira listened as Ozias spoke. His words reminded her of Damisiah. Solomon had told her that the fourth princess, Damisiah, had power over the dead and could hear their song. Was Ozias one of her people?

"Can the living hear the song?" Oadira asked.

"I guess, but the Demirrian bloodlines were wiped out. Only the Ennead can hear them now," Ozias said softly. "The Ennead will now come and take his body."

"The Ennead? Will they really take his body? Why?"

"I am not sure, but they showed up and started collecting dead bodies, a task reserved for the death reclaimers from Naharis's realm. They were all wiped out," Ozias explained.

Oadira held the man as all warmth quickly left his corpse.

“Oadira, we need to go,” Ozias urged. “I know you want what’s best for this man, but what’s best for all the rest of these people is for us to get to safety. Out in the open, the still-cold winds will freeze us instantly.”

Odira nodded, called to the refugees to follow them, and left the man to be covered in snow as his impromptu burial.

They traveled for several hours until torches began dancing ahead in the snow.

“What is that,” Oadira asked.

Ozias grinned. “Family.”

A contingent of Ozias’s people stepped through the wind and swirling flakes, tall and strong like their brother, wearing capes of animal hide and furs on their shoulders. A swarm of friendly faces received the struggling refugees, placing their own pe;ts on the weary newcomers.

A beautiful young woman standing about six-foot-five with a waterfall of black hair extending to her lower back, a hint of violet in her distinguishable eyes, walked up next to Ozias and Oadira.

“How was the mission?” the woman asked.

“A complete failure, Lyshyla,” Ozias said.

“How so?” Lyshyla asked.

“Because of her,” Ozias said, pointing to Oadira. “She shape-shifted into an older Alkebulan woman dying right before me. She then snuck onto one of the ships, sending the dying enslaved to Iceoth to be hunted for sport by the Dalean colonial soldiers.”

“Because of me?” Oadira asked, looking Ozias directly in the face.

“Hmmm.” Lyshyla looked back and forth between Ozias

and Oadira.

"We need to get these people to shelter," Lyshyla shouted to several of the men helping the freezing slaves. "Let's get them over the ridge to the hidden entrance." She turned back toward Ozias. "We'll talk more once we're out of the elements."

The group moved as a unit over a bank of snowy ground almost 500 feet high. The winds whipped more furiously all around them.

"You shape-shifted?" Lyshyla asked Oadira as they came to the crest of the ridge.

"It just happened, involuntarily, without any of my control," Oadira said.

"You had no control over your body and its functions?" Lyshyla asked.

"No," Oadira said.

"Let's get inside. The night will be upon us soon," Lyshyla suggested.

"Where are we heading?" Oadira asked.

"The inner city," Ozias replied.

"The inner city? Where's that? Isn't Iceoth nothing but an icy continent devoid of life?"

Ozias huffed. "I told you my people lived here secretly. We are on our way to Benin City."

"Benin City?" asked Oadira as a gust of wind almost knocked her back.

"That's where my father, Nilhist, is king," said Ozias. The snow flurries turned blizzard-like before Ozias could finish his sentence, darkening the skies and exacerbating the cold.

"Wait," Odira said as snowflakes pummeled her cheeks.

"Your father is the king? That means you're a---"

"The weather is changing," Lyshyla interrupted as she glanced at Oadira. "We're here." She turned back to Ozias. "The rivers aren't flowing as strongly as in years past during this season. It's weighing on your father's mind. Let's go."

Oadira stared into the tempestuous atmosphere in complete amazement. She observed with her protruding cerulean eyes and studied the towering resplendence of the snow-covered trees. They marched along a path of ice that seemed to appear through the snow at their feet. A shaft of sunlight broke through the clouds, sparkling against a city of glass before them. Hundreds of small lakes clustered side by side, along with towers of crystal forming buildings and palaces. It was as if someone had replaced every brick in Londone with a block of ice. The air seemed suddenly warmer and more pleasant, removing the chill that had crept into Oadira's fingers. She was tempted to remove the strip of cloth covering her head and lower face but decided against it. No need to reveal too much about herself just yet. Ozias already knew too much, and she had grown less trusting of him with each encounter. His humility seemed to ebb depending on his mood, and she had no interest in finding out what his state of mind would be once they entered his home city.

"This place is magnificent," Oadira admitted.

"The city of Benin has remained a secret for longer than my lifetime," Ozias said. He seemed pleased with Oadira's reaction to his home. "The hemmed lakes are tied to the farms we use to feed ourselves and the refugees who have stumbled into the city through the years seeking shelter and a new home."

"We're not the first to arrive here?" Oadira asked.

"No," Lyshyla answered. "Many have come, but far fewer arrive than those that set out in the first place."

"When the refugees come in from the boats," Ozias nodded, "most no longer have the ability to work or care for themselves because their bodies have broken down. They find their way here through desperation and whispered tales."

"I helped start a rebellion," Oadira said. "It hurts my heart to see people who no longer have the will to fight."

"Everyone, stop!" Lyshyla shouted, putting her arms over her head. "All of you will stay here outside the city. You will be cared for. Rest for a moment while we discuss matters further."

Oadira grabbed Oazias' arm. "Why aren't they being let into the city?"

"The remaining refugees will not be permitted to enter Benin City per the king's orders," Ozias said as if rehearsing a line from a play. "They are to work the farms to produce food for the citizens of Benin. That's how it's always been."

"What would make someone want to treat people this way?" Oadira asked with a confused look on her face.

"The witan people see and treat these refugees like animals," Ozias shrugged. "The colonial soldiers feel justified hunting them for sport and using them as target practice. They barely think for themselves because of this. They work and survive. That's what they've always done. That's why the king has ordered them outside the city."

"And you think you're better than them?" Oadira shouted. "They've been treated like animals, so they deserve to be worked like animals?"

Lyshyla stepped between Oadira and Ozias, looking Oadira in the eye. "This is a harsh land. We've survived because we make the best decision for the greatest number of people. The fastest way for a city to die is to sacrifice the good of the group to satisfy the emotions of the weak. Because of the rebellion that I understand from the whispers of the huddled men and women back there, you started, there will be more refugees. Because of your actions, they will die if they come here. We can't save everyone. And neither can you. Come with us."

Lyshyla led Oadira, Ozias, and several of the men that helped the refugees, into the city of Benin. As they drew closer, Oadira began to notice that many of the buildings were not as pristine as they appeared from a distance. Part of the city seemed crumbled and dilapidated.

"Why are parts of the city damaged?" Oadira asked. "From a distance it looked so ethereal. Up close it seems much more…broken."

"Centuries ago, Iceoth suffered destruction due to bombardment and multiple invasions at the hands of the colonial forces," Lyshyla said as they passed a broken section of piled ice blocks. "They felt that the people here were a threat to their way of life and wanted to keep them from rising to power. Since then, the colonial powers have lost all knowledge about this place. We've done our best to erase Benin City from their history books. The city is now hidden and unknown to all witans. We honor the devastation of the past by leaving some of the unused sections of the city as they were after that initial attack. It reminds us to be ever vigilant and to trust no outsiders."

Trust no outsiders. And who was Oadira but an outsider? And Ozias was a prince? No wonder he was so pompous. He seemed to care very little for anyone from outside his odd ice kingdom. Oadira knew Solomon had a reason to send her to Iceoth, but with the maps and instructions destroyed in the fire, she had very little to go on. She had no desire to live with these hidden people. They seemed to care only for their own safety and no one else's.

After making their way through Benin, they came to the

center of the city and stood beneath a magnificent palace. Made of ivory stone, lined with deep grays and light blues, the citadel and its spires towered into the wintry sky, a crowning testament to the city's once-regal standing. Positioned outside the palace, before the curved set of stairs that led to the entrance, was a large ice-stone throne. Seated on the throne was a large man, seven feet tall with great muscular definition. He wore dreadlocks weaved into one long, rope-like braid that ran down the middle of his back and had bulky legs and ivory teeth that sparkled. He appeared regal and kingly, capturing Oadira's attention. Armed guards surrounded him, along with advisors dressed in robes, and voluntary servants who lingered nearby.

"Behold!" a crier in a blue cape shouted as the group approached. "King Nilhist, of the throne of Benin. Let all who come near, respect his throne, and speak only when addressed by his majesty."

Ozias and Lyshyla both bowed. Oadira copied their movements. She had never stood before a real king before, at least that she could remember. The entire scene seemed strange and foreign.

"Son, you have returned. How was your journey?" asked King Nilhist with a nod toward Ozias.

Ozias lowered to one knee and bowed his head. "Father, I have failed," he said.

So, it was true. Ozias was a prince. Oadira stayed quiet, arms folded in irritation.

"Do you remember what your objective was?" King Nilhist asked.

"Yes, Father, but while on the mission, things just kind of…changed," said Ozias.

"Explain!" King Nilhist ordered.

"I couldn't locate and dispose of Madame Lalaurie. The intel was wrong. She wasn't where she was supposed to be. Due to the rebellions, I aborted and waited until the ships docked, bringing me back to Iceoth. I ran into this woman afterward."

"Wait," Oadira shouted. "You were trying to kill Madame…"

"Silence!" the crier bellowed. "You will speak when spoken to, outsider!"

King Nihilist's eyes cut to Oadira. "Who is this young woman you've brought to Iceoth to stand before me?"

"Oadira," Ozias said, still kneeling. He gestured to Oadira, who stood to his right, cloaked by the cloth she had torn from the bottom of her dress.

"Remove your garb, woman," commanded King Nilhist. Oadira did as instructed and removed her makeshift head scarf. The king gasped, reacting to Oadira's cerulean eyes and blue hair. He stared at her with deepening curiosity. Flabbergasted, he stuttered as he spoke.

"You are…"

"I am what?" Odira asked, frustration evident in her voice.

"You are Sahaelian royalty," King Nilhist said, swallowing.

"I am," Oadira nodded.

"I didn't know at first, Father," Ozias said, coming to his feet. "Her eyes weren't blue before, and her hair only had a hint of blue to it. It wasn't until we jumped into the water---"

"When you stepped off of the ship," King Nilhist interrupted. "Did you expose your eyes to the sea, Daughter of Sahael?"

"Yes," replied Oadira apprehensively.

King Nilhist grew quiet, sitting back on his ice-stone throne. "The Signs of the Times are upon us." He brought his hand up to his face to scratch his cheek. "Oadira, is it? You are welcome to stay here as long as you want until you are needed elsewhere." King Nilhist waved his hand. "Ladies of the court; you are to care for this woman as though she were our own. She is tired and hungry, I would guess. Take care of her and we will speak again soon."

The ladies of the court embraced Oadira and welcomed her openly.

Exiting the presence of King Nilhist and Ozias, the ladies escorted Oadira around Benin City, ending their tour at the guest chamber where Oadira would stay for the remainder of her visit. The hospitality of the women filled her with warmth, but conflicted emotions settled in her mind. She was overjoyed with being around those who wanted to be left alone to live peacefully, but she was dismayed and confused regarding her path forward. She wanted to know more about Prince Ozias, yet she knew their time together would be brief. Her bedchamber was inviting and cozy, meager yet exquisite. But much like her time with Madame Lalaurie, she sat in luxury while her people worked and toiled outside the city. She had traded one locked door for another.

Fatigue from her journey overcame her, and outside of a nice, satiating meal, she wanted nothing more than sleep. Soon, it found her.

After a few days of settling in, Oadira became well acquainted with the city and its people. During this time, Oadira developed an intentional and friendly relationship with Ozias. She knew that if she were to help her people currently working the farms outside the city, she would need to find favor in the king's sight, and Ozias was the quickest way to accomplish that.

"How are you settling in?" Ozias asked Oadira as they

walked the shore around one of the lakes. He wore a royal cloak with fur fringes. Oadira's clothing was similar, warm yet not too bulky that she couldn't run or fight if needed.

"I'm getting along," she answered. "I'm comfortable, if that's what you're asking."

"It is. I was hoping you could join my father and I for dinner this evening."

"I can't," Oadira smiled. "I'll be outside the city working with the escaped slaves of Sahael. They are growing stronger, yet they still feel trapped. I feel the same, to a certain extent."

Ozias stopped and turned toward Oadira. "You're not trapped, Princess. You have free access to the entire city."

"And yet my people do not," Oadira replied. "More and more I'm coming to realize that if my people aren't free, I'm not free. Even six months ago I would have run off at the first chance and never looked back. That was before I knew who I was. Now that I do, I can't let my people suffer. You've been kind to let the refugees stay here and work, but they'll never be anything more than outsiders and slaves to you."

"That's not true," Ozias said. A sadness came to his eyes. He glanced at his feet and then looked back up at Oadira. "Here in Benin, life isn't easy. We may not be slaves, but we're in a constant state of survival. My servant and best friend, Ossa, and I have worked since we were children to uphold the safety of this land, as my father did before us. We don't have the population to withstand an assault by the witan governments if they discovered our location. We don't have enough food to sustain many more people. I see how you care for those under your charge. I do. Honestly, I wish I could see them the way you do."

Oadira touched his hand. "Then come with me and see them for yourself. Get to know them, not from next to your father's throne, but by my side."

A smile brightened Oazias' face and he agreed. The two royal children spent the rest of the day working and serving among the refugees. The people smiled at them both, talking about their trials as slaves and saying they were happy to be free of the Lalaurie estate. Some of them had been slaves in other lands as well, bought and sold numerous times over the years. Ozias seemed to listen intently, mentioning at one point he hadn't known the trials people had suffered until his mission to the colonies.

As Oadira and Ozias walked back to the city at dusk, Oadira felt it was a good moment for more questions. Their feet crunched quietly in the snow, no other sound seemingly reaching their ears.

"Why did you want to kill Madame Lalaurie?" she asked.

"My father wanted her dead," Ozias admitted.

"Why?"

Ozias took a deep breath. "Too many refugees have been finding their way here over the past few years. Stories are still told of a hidden land on Iceoth, and the desperate people will take any hope they can find. We sent spies to discover what might happen if one of the more powerful slave matrons was murdered. They decided it would spread chaos and give escaping slaves a reason to go elsewhere. If they hope of escaping more easily to more hospitable lands, we would no longer have to worry about excess mouths to feed."

"And you were going to kill her the night of the rebellion," Oadira stated.

"Within the next few days, for certain," Ozias said, taking a few steps forward along the lake's edge. "I had learned her movements and where she would likely be at any given time. I had heard rumors during my weeks hiding amongst the slaves in the northern plantations about a rebellion, but I didn't think anyone could inspire them to fight back. I hadn't met you yet, of course."

"Sorry I wrecked your assassination plot," Oadira smiled.

Ozias nudged her playfully with his shoulder. "Well, I did place the blame squarely on you when my father asked about it, like a coward, so I would say we're even."

"I wouldn't say you're a coward, Ozias."

"You wouldn't?"

Oadira nudged him back, making him trip slightly and catch himself. "Pompous, yes. A coward? No."

Over the next few days, Oadira and Ozias began spending more time together under the watchful eye of King Nilhist and his guards. Oadira wasn't sure whether or not the king appreciated their growing friendship. He often made excuses to keep them apart. The king would mention how Oadira was the catalyst of the unprecedented change affecting the lands, and he knew that her emergence was either an omen or a godsend.

It was obvious the king wasn't sure whether Oadira's presence was good or bad. That being the case, he rarely interacted with her directly, and didn't seem happy in her spending time with Ozias. Each day several guards would follow them, not closely, but close enough to be noticeable.

The king's thinly veiled effort to keep them apart was in vain though, as they spent more and more time together. Some days, Ozias would even exit the city to work and talk with the former slaves long before Oadira had a chance to meet him there.

He seemed to enjoy his time picking berries and harvesting sweet grasses from the lake shores with the men and women of the plantations. He laughed more easily and shared stories of Iceoth with the children.

Oadira and Ozias began spending hours at the library, reading about the past and learning the history of Iceoth so she could share the stories as well. The library was old with rock-made aisles that held a few hundred books, a small record of their short history. Dust, cobwebs, and dirt seemed to cover everything. Candles placed in lamps glowed all around them. In the center of the library were some tables and chairs for sitting, and that became the pair's base of operation.

On their third day of studying in the library, Oadira noticed the cast-iron statue of a man in a lunging position, one hand on a conch shell and the other stretched out in front of him. The man looked as if he were alerting others to some cause or raising an alarm. Oadira read the small inscription on the base: *The souls of our people will never break.*

"That's a beautiful inscription on that statue," Oadira said, closing a book and turning to face the statue more directly. "What does it mean?"

"This is a sacred story to my people," Ozias said, leaning back in his chair. "The story of the slave, Neg Mawon, who helped liberate Iceoth by assembling his tribesmen, the only pure-blooded tribe existing in Iceoth."

Ozias handed Oadira a large history book and opened to the image of the statue with a brief description underneath. Oadira read from the book.

"*Seventy of the men and women in Iceoth were born free people, hailing from the far reaches of Alkebulan and Sahael. As testaments to his sacrifice, leadership, and victory, they symbolized his epic struggle of breaking obsidian chains that once kept him shackled. Machete in hand, defiant and unafraid, blowing the conch to call others to freedom, Neg Mawon's victory resulted in Iceoth's bitter attacks by witan colonials for over three hundred years.* That is a really good story. How long have your people been in Iceoth?"

"As long as I can remember. They began taming this land the moment the colonial armies arrived," said Prince Ozias. "We continually have to fight against the Dales, who enslaved our people until my great-great-great-great-grandfather, Neg Mawon, broke his obsidian chains with his bare hands. That played a pivotal role, in that everyone could hear the breaking of his chains. The sound of freedom reverberated in their ears. Many joined in his rebellion because they refused enslavement. The Dalean forces retreated to the colonies and chose to remain in isolation. It's been generations since they've come inland enough to find the city. We hunt their spies regularly to this day. That is why our safety is a constant concern. The more people that come here, the more likely it is for the Dales to discover us and to alert other nations. It is all in the history of our people," Ozias said.

Oadira listened, gazing at the statue and the volumes of texts.

"Solomon told me to come here," she said slowly. "He said this was the next step in my journey. He told me about gates to other parts of Aarde that would lead me to Sahael, but his maps were lost in the fire that destroyed Madame Lalaurie's estate house. He told me his instructions would make sense once I arrived in Iceoth, but I don't have those instructions anymore, so I'm lost and blind. Do you know of any gates, Nairohenge or Medjay? Does that sound familiar?"

Ozias shook his head. "It doesn't. I'm sorry."

"I still don't know what to do, honestly," Oadira breathed. "The past few weeks have been eye-opening, but I feel no closer to finding answers. I wonder what books need to be studied and which pages need to be read to help provide me clues that could help me get to Sahael."

"What do you know about your people?" Ozias asked.

"Very little, beyond what Solomon told me and my cousins after the Royal Rumble months ago. I have not been able to find anything beyond that. What do you know of Sahael?"

"Not much. My people once lived there, but that was centuries ago, before even my father was born."

A tall attractive man with dreadlocks in his hair, wearing the black and blue cloak of a palace servant, entered the room quietly.

"Lord Ozias," the man said with a bow.

"You don't have to call me that, Ossa," Ozias chuckled. "My father isn't in earshot."

Ossa grinned bright white teeth against his dark skin. "Fine, Lord Dung Rat. Lyshyla wants to see you."

Ozias stood and bowed toward Oadira. "I've got to go, but feel free to read whatever you want. Ossa, stay behind and help Oadira find the books she needs."

"Most of them aren't here anymore, Ozias," Ossa said, motioning toward the empty shelves along the back walls of the library.

"I know," Ozias nodded. "Just help her find what you can."

From that day on, Oadira started reading all the books in the small library, grabbing a chair each morning, and sitting across from Ozias as he joined in her quest for clues. Ossa would bring them food and make fun of Ozias on occasion, making Oadira laugh. In the afternoons she and the prince would visit the Sahaelians outside the city and make sure they were comfortable and fed. At times the food from their meager harvests would be barely enough to sustain them and the citizens of Benin, but by the grace of the gods, no one starved as the snow seemed to grow harsher as the season progressed.

One dark morning Oadira sat alone beside a candle in the library, reading about Ibeji's blessing of long life, and how King Nilhist had fought at the head of an Iceoth army that supposedly had battled over a century before.

"What are you looking for today?" Ozias asked as he walked in with a platter of berries and roasted Tremor meat.

"Same thing as always," Oadira replied. "I know you brought me here to learn more stories for the children, but now I feel like I need to know this history, not just of Iceoth, but of all our people. I did just find an interesting passage though. It talks about your father fighting in a battle over a century ago. Did one of your ancestors have his same name?"

Ozias placed the platter in front of Oadira and took a quick bite of Tremor meat. "No, it was him. Nearly three hundred years ago in the ice caverns of Iceoth, my father became king but decided to leave the caverns and rebuild the city of Benin. For the last one hundred years, we have had to fight off Dalean forces and take refugees into the city to look after and care for them. My father's line, and thus my line, are the only remnants of the ancient blood who share the benefits of extended life per Ibeji's blessings."

"So how old is your dad?" Oadira asked. He looked to be middle-aged, no older.

"342."

Amazing. Oadira had heard stories as a child of ancient people living for centuries, but to actually meet one and know of the reality of that tale made her heart beat faster. And if King Nilhist was over 300 years old, what did that say about Ozias?

"How old are you?" she asked.

"I am young," Ozias smiled. "My father didn't marry my mother until he was already of-age. You can ask Ossa if you don't believe me. He'll tell you the truth."

"So, your father was there when this city was last assaulted," Oadira said.

"He was." Ozias took a deep breath as he maintained eye contact with Oadira. "I told you the Daleans don't know about this city, which is true, but my people were sent to the other cities to help rebuild them. My father wanted to keep the main city protected at all costs. The surrounding cities were set up to be found by Dalean forces. Many of the refugees we take in are actually sent to those other cities."

Sent to other cities? Sent to be targets for aggression so the people here in Benin could be safe? Oadira's cheek twitched as she tried to keep her temper under control.

"Sent to die in attacks by the Daleans so this city can remain hidden," Oadira spat, slamming the book closed. "Are these your father's orders?"

"Yes. The outer cities were initially used as barriers while the people rebuilt. They also served as a warning and the first lines of defense to allow the people in the inner city to escape," Ozias said candidly.

Oadira got up from the old wooden table quickly. "That doesn't sound right to me!"

"I know it is not right, but my father made it so per the guidance of the Chosen Bloodlines. They didn't want to put the bloodline of the Ancient Order at risk." Ozias slumped over the table.

"What's the Ancient Order?" she asked, folding her arms and looking at Ozias. "Why is it so important that you'd send people to be sacrificed without them even knowing?"

"To be honest, I don't really know that much except that they consist of the four bloodlines: the Orishan bloodline, the Hausan bloodline, the Yoruban bloodline, and the Demirrian bloodline."

Oadira had heard these names before, from Solomon. If Ozias knew about them, there had to be more records somewhere in this city that would tell her what she needed to know.

"What more can you tell me about these four bloodlines?" she asked.

"I only know about the Orishan bloodline," Ozias said.

"How come? You're a prince, aren't you?"

Ozias stood up from the table. "I don't know! This is all that the library has to offer. What you see here has been placed curated selectively over time. My father refuses to talk about it. I have spent years searching and that has led to very little information."

"Are there no other books?" Oadira asked.

"Every book was sent to the archives in the caves per the orders of my father," said Ozias with a casual wave, as if the books had been thrown away.

"Why is that?" Oadira asked.

"I don't know. We don't ask questions." Ozias looked at the stone floor. "I don't ask questions."

Oadira walked up to Ozias and put her hands on his shoulders. "Is it possible for us to travel to the caverns and take a look at those archives?"

Ozias looked Oadira directly in her eyes. "It's impossible."

"Why?" Oadira asked.

"There is no way to get there from here, from anywhere in the city, or from the royal quarters. It's heavily guarded; all are restricted from entering," Ozias said.

"Your father is hiding something he doesn't want you to find."

"My father issued a series of laws forbidding anyone from ever entering the caverns years ago. The Anubis warriors remain in the cavern to keep anyone from entering."

"Why do you think that is?" Oadira asked, voice rising.

"Over three hundred years of my bloodline's history is there," Ozias said. "I need to respect my father's wishes."

Oadira looked Ozias in the eye, doing her best to remain calm. She needed to read those records. What began as a way for her to learn more stories to share with children had turned into a search that could lead her to Sahael. This may have been the very reason Solomon sent her to Iceoth in the first place.

"Answer me this," Oadira said calmly. "If I weren't here, would you have sent the slaves that escaped from the ships with us to those other cities to likely be killed by Daleans?"

"If you weren't here," Ozias said slowly, "they would have been left to die on the frozen shores of this land. You knew that already. I've never tried to hide anything from you. This is a harsh land, and our ways sometimes must be harsh."

"You're hiding something from me now," Oadira replied. "You're hiding the knowledge I may need to unite our peoples. It may lead to me learning more about where we all come from, and how to get into Sahael safely."

"Oadira, we just can't," Ozias said.

Letting her shoulders slump, Oadira let her posture soften. She could feel Ozias' desire to learn more. He wasn't a fool. "Aren't you curious to know more about your people, and maybe find out why your father is so intent on keeping that knowledge from everyone; why he passed a law that takes away knowledge from his own people?"

"My father issued the law after the death of my mother," said Ozias softly.

"Oh, I'm . . . I'm sorry. I never meant to push," Oadira said.

"It's okay, and there is no way you could have known," Ozias said sadly. "My mother, Queen Nilda, had blue eyes like you. She died in the caverns as the structures built by the people caved in. My father dug out the areas inside the cavern and never found her body."

Odira stepped closer, placing her hand on his neck, and rubbing lightly. "It seems the death of your mother has caused you and your father a lot of pain."

"It has," Ozias said. Tears came to his eyes, but Oadira could tell he was fighting against his emotions like a dam holding back an ocean. "My father never speaks of my mother anymore. He has bathed in anger and darkness since then."

"I understand your pain…and his," Oadira said. She dropped her hand from his neck and grasped his hand with her own. "My own mother died when I was very young. She gave her life to ensure my safety after Natas invaded Sahael. She sacrificed her life so I could live." Holding up the bracelet on her wrist, Oadira continued. "Her essence is now in this bracelet, always to guide and protect me. Natas killed them, thinking the Ancient Bloodline was severed forever. Sahael is my home. I must find a way back. If I can learn anything from your father's hidden records, I will sacrifice what I need in order to do so."

The two of them stood in silence for a moment. Oadira took a few barriers from the platter and chewed them slowly. She needed access to those records. If Ozias wouldn't help her, she would find a way herself.

"I need a moment. I'll be right back," Ozias said.

He left the library, but after only a few minutes, he reentered, making eye contact with Oadira once again.

"The only way we can get to the caverns is by traveling outside of the city to avoid all of my father's guards," Ozias said.

Oadira tried to suppress a grin but was unsuccessful. "How do you know that?"

"My father told me everything to get in and out of the city in case of emergencies," Ozias said. "I've trained with the sentinels who stand guard over the cavern entrance as well."

"How will we be able to make it out of the city without your father's guards following us and watching every move we make?" asked Oadira. "It seems like every day he puts more of his soldiers on alert to watch us."

"I know. They're outside the library right now as always."

"Then what do we do?"

"I have an idea," said Ozias, huddling close to Oadira as if every word they spoke was now being overheard. "Under the cover of night, we can sneak out. That is the only time the guards will have their shift changes. During that time, we'll make our way toward the outskirts of the city."

"Where exactly?" Oadira asked.

"The location where we first met Lyshyla," Ozias said.

Oadira thought to herself for a moment as she tried to remember. "Over the ridge beyond the lakes," she whispered. "Are we really going to do this?"

"If you're in, I'm in."

Without a moment's thought, Oadira gave Ozias a kiss on the cheek, startling him.

He blinked, cheeks pulling up into a slight smile.

Suddenly, they lunged toward each other and kissed, lips locked for a few seconds. They were quickly interrupted as one of the guards' boots could be heard walking down the hall toward the sitting area.

"Lord Ozias," the man called in a deep voice.

"Yes, Ossa?" Ozias answered, pulling away from Oadira.

Ossa stepped into view; dark face lit up by the candles on the wall next to the bookshelves. "The king is ordering you and Princess Oadira to the throne room. I have come as your escort." He paused, looking at the two of them as they breathed heavily, Oadira sitting awkwardly on the table next to Ozias. "Is everything alright?"

"We're fine, Ossa," Ozias answered, feigning ignorance. "We were just reading about Iceoth history and got excited about teaching the refugee children. That's all."

"I'm sure," Ossa grinned.

Ossa led Ozias and Oadira outside the library where the guards stood at attention. They seemed nervous, as if they had been reprimanded for some reason. Oadira assumed it was because they had allowed the two royals to study alone without chaperones. Ozias had convinced them days ago that guarding him was not necessary in the library, but Oadira figured they would not get much privacy after today.

"Did you see the looks on the guards' faces outside the library?" Ozias whispered to Oadira as they walked toward the palace behind Ossa.

"They looked like someone had just screamed at them," she replied.

"Someone did," Ossa replied, looking back at them. "As I approached the library, General Kiuta was reprimanding them for not joining to two of you in the library. Apparently, your father is unhappy with how much time you are spending together."

"And what do you think, Ossa?" Oadira asked with pleasant cadence.

Ossa shrugged. "I think my friend Ozias is less pompous when you're around."

Ozias slugged Ossa in the arm playfully. "Oh, that's what you think?"

"It is, oh great prince of Benin."

"All of my movements are watched by people who have nothing better to do except make my life miserable," said Ozias. "At least they've been discreet till now. I'm betting they're going to be watching us more closely from here on out."

"I would assume so," Ossa nodded.

They entered the palace, Ossa leading them down a long stone hall with tapestries hanging from ceiling to floor. They entered a banquet room anchored by a large stone table that could easily seat twenty people. King Nilhist sat alone, biting into a roasted animal leg before taking a drink from a crystal goblet.

"You wanted to see us, Father," Ozias said, back straight.

"I take it your 'studying' is going well in the library?" The king drawled, still chewing his meat.

"It is, Father. I've been teaching Oadira our historic tales to tell the refugee children outside the city. They enjoy our stories so much."

"I'm sure they do," the king nodded. "They've been eating enough of our food, after all."

"Your highness…" Oadira began, stepping forward.

"You may go, Princess Oadira," the king interrupted. "I would speak with my son alone."

"Yes, your highness," Oadira said. She looked at Ozias before turning to leave. She had only made it a few steps when the king's voice echoed through the large hall.

"My guards will watch you closely and report every little thing that you do."

Oadira looked over her shoulder and nodded. "I understand, King Nilhist. I have no desire to offend you in any way."

"I'm sure," the king replied, eyes focused on the food in front of him.

Oadira returned to her quarters and sat on the bed. The king was obviously not happy with her presence in Benin. While he had at first appeared content to let circumstances play out, Nilhist now seemed eager to control Oadira's very movements in the city. What would Ozias do if his father ordered him to cut off all contact with Oadira, or worse, he told his father about their plans to try and infiltrate the archives? Would the ruler take it out on the refugees currently working on the farms outside the city? Oadira didn't doubt it.

And now she had kissed Ozias too. She had grown fond of him over the past few weeks, particularly seeing him with the children, or the times he would work alongside the freed slaves in the berry fields. He was handsome, strong, surprisingly thoughtful, and had shown vulnerability. Much of the arrogance Oadira had seen in him appeared to be more of a mask than anything else. He seemed to legitimately enjoy working with the people and studying history. Oadira bet that if push came to shove, he would defend the refugees right alongside her.

She liked him.

She had liked kissing him.

When night fell upon the city, Oadira watched fires alight across the area below her window. Oil from the sweet grasses burned yellow with sparkles of green in basins up and down the stone streets of Benin.

A light knock pulled her gaze to her front door. It opened before she could stand up from her bed.

"Oadira," Ozias said with a smile.

"Ozias! What are you doing here?"

He took her hand and squeezed it. "If we want to get into the caverns and look at the records, tonight is our last chance. Father is doubling the guards on both of us and has ordered me to keep my distance from you. He's become paranoid about this entire situation. He no longer believes the signs of the times are good. I couldn't convince him otherwise. I snuck out of my room and came directly here. I actually climbed through the side window on the second landing to make sure no one saw me. the guard shift is going to change within the next few minutes."

Oadira turned and grabbed her fur cape from the chair next to her mirror. "Then we better get going."

Ozias and Oadira waited in her quarters until the guard shift took effect. They then climbed through the second landing window and moved through the city individually, taking different paths to meet at their agreed location. Oadira arrived first and stood in front of an ice sculpture of a siren, waiting for Ozias. The night was cold as always, but clear and inviting. Stars danced overhead.

"Oadira," Ozias whispered softly from the dark alley to her left.

Oadira heard his voice and, with excitement, hurried over to where Ozias was hiding, smiling from ear to ear.

"Were you followed?" Ozias asked.

"I don't believe so," Oadira said.

Ozias' smile matched Oadira's. "Then let us get going."

CHAPTER IV

THE ICE CAVERNS OF ICEOTH

Iceoth, Benin City, The Caverns

Ozias and Oadira traveled the entire night, stumbling upon a small, undeveloped city during their trek. In the darkness, Oadira saw a camp of Dalean soldiers next to a wall of ice. Bodies lie on the frozen ground all around, both witans and Alkebulans. A battle had obviously taken place here the day before, and Oadira wondered how many fresh refugees had died here, never knowing they were protecting a city they didn't even know existed. Ozias and Oadira crept silently through the area, retreating deep into the canyonlands and walking along the snowy rivers. At one point a family of ice turtles jumped from the water and chased them from the city into the wilderness.

"Where are we?" Oadira asked as dawn approached. She was tired and cold but elated they had made it this far.

"We've arrived in Kuma," said Ozias as they squatted behind a sizable boulder. The sun rose in front of them. "Look at the ridgeline there. See anything?"

Odira squinted against the sun to the east, seeing a collection of stone buildings that blended into the white hills around them. "There's a town there. Are we going to interact with the people?"

"No, my father's guards are here. Within a few hours they'll know you and I are gone from Benin and start looking for us. Word will reach Kuma by midmorning. It's best no one knows we came near here. We need to get out of the area as quickly as we can."

"Good idea," Oadira said.

They crept back to the snowy river, making their way up to the snow canyon. They walked a few hours until they encountered Oth-Lake, which consisted of multiple streams, rivers, and reservoirs that fed into the lake, along with a large, gushing waterfall. Oadira stopped and took in the most gorgeous scenery her blue eyes had ever witnessed.

"What a beautiful sight to see—this lake teeming with fish, circled by snow-covered land, keeping it all encased and secluded," Oadira said.

"This is a sacred place for me," Ozias said. "Whenever I've had interactions with Oth-Lake, my eyes always turn blue like yours, and tattoos appear on my body."

"How is that possible?" Oadira asked. "Why didn't you ever tell me that before?"

Ozias shrugged. "I'm not the only one affected in this way. My mother didn't even have the same reaction in these waters. I told you back on the ship that I had seen glowing blue eyes before. Whenever I dip my head in the water…I'll show you. Let's both do it."

Kneeling at the lake's edge, Ozias dipped his head below the surface. His eyes lit up, matching Oadira's, and tribal tattoos appeared on his shoulders and arms. Oadira did the same, dipping her head into the crisp cold waters. Her eyes and skin reacted in the same way as Ozias. Her own tattoos glowed blue. She laughed, feeling a connection to Ozias that she had never felt with anyone before. He was like her, a remnant of the Sahaelian bloodline, lost in a dangerous and hateful world.

The two of them sat for a while in the quiet solitude as Ozias' tattoos and blue eyes faded. Oadira's stayed bright as always. Ozias focused on the waterfall across the lake.

"Something isn't right," Ozias said, eyes squinting.

"What is it?"

"Oth-Lake is flowing in the opposite direction than it usually does," he said.

"Is that bad?" asked Oadira. She looked at the waters, but they seemed normal, flowing toward the north, away from the waterfall.

"Yes, it's bad," Ozias said. He stood up and focused on the waterfall. "If the flow in Oth-Lake is reversed, the lake will stop generating food for the island of Iceoth and its inhabitants. Lyshyla mentioned the weather had changed and that less water was flowing from the upper lakes."

"I don't understand," Oadira said.

"The waterfall powers the flow that creates the current, which powers the rivers, ensuring food flows throughout Iceoth. If the flow has stopped, or changed directions, the currents have reversed, which means the rivers will stop flowing because the water will go to the ocean instead of the interior. The island will slowly die." Ozias looked to the sky and breathed deeply. "The Signs of the Times."

"What do you mean?" Oadira asked. "I thought The Signs of the Times meant we would be returning to Sahael."

"It means a lot of things," Ozias whispered without looking at Oadira. "My father spoke to me of change last night. If what he assumes is true, and the reversing of the lake's flow would back that up, it's time for the people to leave Iceoth. Benin City and everything we've fought for will die."

Oadira bent down and placed her hand in the water. When she was in the ocean after jumping from the ship, she could feel the currents and pull of the water. Closing her eyes, she allowed her senses to attune to the water itself and feel the tug of the ocean.

"I can feel the current and the source of where the flow has shifted," she said. "Follow me."

They ran around the lake to where the waterfall impacted the surface. A half mile from the cataract, water spilled over a ridge that looked out on a collection of icy boulders below them, along with a frosted landscape and the ocean far in the distance. A second waterfall spilled over the crest, forming a river that made its way to the coast, siphoning water from the lake.

"By Ishtar," Ozias whispered.

"What is it?"

Ozias pointed toward the waterfall at their feet and up at the horizon. "The last time I was here there was a wall of ice along where this ridgeline is. At some point in the last year that wall must have shattered. Look below us. Those boulders of ice are all that remain. As more of this ridge melts, more water will flow from the lake here on the east side, meaning eventually no water will reach Benin at all."

A deep sadness seemed to press on Ozias' shoulders. They slumped, and his entire posture seemed to shrink.

Oadira wanted to comfort him but had no idea what to say. If what Ozias said was true, his people's entire way of life was about to be obliterated.

“Look out there,” Ozias said, pointing toward the coastline. “You see the ships out there?”

Squinting, Odira made out the shapes of white sales, as well as what looked like tiny ants moving across the white shoreline.

“Those are Dalean ships,” Ozias said. “They’re dropping off troops. I can tell even from this distance by the formations they’re using. All the ice that used to make that bay impassable is now gone. They may well be setting camp for an invasion of the continent.”

More good news, thought Oadira. She had barely escaped slavery and death, only to land on a frozen continent where the most powerful people had no desire to help anyone, and only wanted to be left alone in secret. She was starting to understand the appeal.

Something white appeared in Oadira’s peripheral vision, just below them among the boulders. Several giant snow spiders, covered in coarse white hair, creeped toward them, each over a foot tall.

“Ozias!” screamed Oadira, pointing at the oversized arachnids blending in with the snowy environment.

“Maybe we triggered one of their webs!” Ozias said. He grabbed Oadira’s arm and pulled her back toward the lake. “Run! They swarm and overwhelm their prey. We could be wrapped up in their webs and helpless in seconds.”

Oadira conjured several throwing daggers, hitting the snow spiders in the eyes as more of them scurried from their hiding places among the shattered ice wall. Soon, dozens of the eight-legged creatures darted towards the fleeing royals.

“We need to get out of here!” Oadira screamed.

Ozias looked at the large waterfall. “Hold your breath!

We're jumping back into the lake. They can't swim. It's our only option."

Holding hands, they held their breath and jumped into the icy water. Icy pinpricks stabbed at Oadira's skin as the cold surrounded her with far more potency than the air had. Above the rippling surface, snow spiders converged on the edge of the lake, spitting web spikes at them through the water. Oadira surfaced to take a breath and instantly had to dash back below as several webs cut through the air trying to ensnare her.

As before, tattoos started to appear on both Ozias's and Oadira's skin. She needed to breathe and knew Ozias couldn't hold his breath much longer either. As her tattoos continued glowing, a peace washed over her. The water's chill dissipated as if her body temperature changed to match the environment. Instinctively, Oadira knew she was safe here in her element. She wanted to taste the water, breathe it in, become one with it, knowing nothing could harm her.

And so, she did.

Oadira released the air from her lungs and breathed deeply of the water. She found, surprisingly, that she didn't need to surface for air. She could breathe underwater, like a fish. A smile filled her face as she finally understood her connection to the liquid world. This was her domain, and she could move between land and water like walking into another room in a house.

Ozias wasn't smiling, however. Eyes wide, he looked to the surface where the spiders still gathered, waiting for their prey to reemerge. He couldn't hold his breath anymore.

Just as Ozias kicked his feet to swim back up for air, Oadira grabbed him and pressed her lips to his. With a great blow of oxygen, she filled his lungs with air she had filtered from the water. He seemed shocked at first, but then calmed himself and stopped fighting, breathing deeply. The two of them floated for some time in the quiet tranquility of the lake, mouths open to each other, breathing silently.

Eventually the spiders seemed to lose interest and scampered off. After waiting a bit longer to be sure, Oadira swam herself and Ozias to the shore.

They scrambled into the gravel beach, both coughing as they climatized to the surface. The air burned warm to Oadira's skin after the comfort of the deep, but Ozias shivered for the first time since they had arrived in Iceoth weeks before.

"How did you…" Ozias coughed. "How did you do that?"

"I don't know," Oadira admitted. "I just knew it. Once we were in the water, it just felt like home. I knew I could breathe, and that I could breathe for you. I don't know how else to describe it."

"Thank you," Ozias said, squeezing Oadira's hand. Water dripped from his nose and lips. "If we had gone back to the surface, the spiders would have snared us in their webs." He looked over his shoulder toward the ridge where the spiders had originally climbed from their hiding places. "We better go now. It's not safe here, and we're close to the caverns at this point. There are warm shafts of thermal air near the entrance to the caverns where we can dry off and get warm again. We won't survive long all wet."

Ozias led Oadira another mile into the hills. The cold returned to her body and after a few minutes, her wet clothing seemed to pull the strength from her limbs. Everywhere they went, Ozias mentioned the change in the environment. Several glaciers had receded north, while barren rock faced the sun where not long before snow and ice had covered.

They came to a crevice leading deep below a cleft of black rock. Warm air and steam rose from cracks in the cliff face.

"We're here," Ozias said. "Let's take a minute to dry off.

The air is quite hot here at the mouth of the crevice."

They rested and basked in the warm blowing vents. Oadira expected to smell sulfur, the air tasted clean and fresh, at times hot enough to burn the skin. Once dry, they put their capes back on.

"I don't know what we're going to find down here in the Nibiru tunnel," Ozias said as he led Oadira into the crevasse. "Normally there's a lot more snow and ice around here, even with the thermal vents. We need to be wary with every step. I've never been any farther than this."

"Do you know where this tunnel will take us?" Oadira asked.

"Only one way to find out," Ozias replied.

Ozias and Oadira entered the Nibiru tunnel and walked until they reached an opening into a large cavern. Along the walls, all they could see was a natural reserve of ice-stone, much like King Nilhist's throne back at Benin City. The walls seemed to glow all around them as if shining with hidden power. The air grew warmer and more humid the farther they traveled. The light grew brighter as well toward the far end of the space. They walked deeper into the cavern through another section of tunnel. When they emerged, Oadira and Ozias found themselves inside an enormous underground cave, encompassing an entire ecosystem large enough to fit multiple cities. Green acres stretched far and wide. A bevy of Marula Tree roots dipped in and out of the ground as their leaves sat as still as the humid air. Clusters of empty wooden homes dotted the area, creating rustic villages with fences and thatched roofs. Strange, arctic animals grazed along the grass and ate fish from the coursing streams that cut through the land. In the center of the cavern stood a pyramid of crystalline ice-stone, giving light to the area as if the sun had been pulled from the sky and buried in the cave underground. The symbol of Ankh, with its teardrop shaped hoop attached to a cross underneath, was painted above the entrance.

"What is this place?" Oadira asked.

"Nearly four hundred years ago, my mother's people built these caverns. They are home to the great ice-stone pyramid that houses the history of all my people," said Ozias, face alight with excitement. "None of us have ever been allowed to come here. I thought the stories my mother told me of this place were a fairytale. It's more amazing than I imagined."

"This is wonderful," Oadira said with excitement.

"Shh!" whispered Ozias, who motioned for Oadira to hide with him. "Did you hear that?"

"I didn't hear anything," Oadira said.

"Footsteps are approaching from both directions."

They looked around for a place to hide, but before they could see any obvious cover, Oadira heard the footsteps as well. Seven-foot-tall Anubis warrior with jackal headdresses, marched from behind a series of boulders to their left. The men were chiseled and muscular, with ebony skin and long, pointed ears. They carried buckler shields and Konda swords marked with a water dragon symbol Oadira recognized from somewhere, all made from Orichalcum. The Anubis warriors consisted of archers, javelinists, and Orishan cavalry.

And there was nowhere for Oadira and Ozias to hide.

Panic struck Oadira's heart. They had come all this way, walked all night and now most of the day, fled from giant spiders, only to be captured the moment they stepped into this sacred place.

To her surprise, the warriors simply walked past Oadira and Ozias as if they weren't even there. They continued walking toward the pyramid, disappearing through the grass and trees.

"The Anubis warriors aren't paying any attention to us.

They're marching to the entrance," Ozias breathed.

"What does that mean?" Oadira whispered.

A dark anger seemed to flame in Ozias' eyes. "It means we're not alone."

He grabbed Oadira's hand and started walking through the tall grass toward the pyramid. Birds chirped in trees overhead as they stumbled upon a path made of ice-stone that led directly toward the triangular structure. They heard voices talking animatedly and stopped next to a Marula tree.

"That's my father's voice," Ozias whispered. "I knew it!"

Oadira peeked from behind the tree and saw a line of soldiers standing next to a large stone entrance at the base of the pyramid. Two other people argued about something behind the legion. Oadira immediately recognized them as King Nilhist and Lyshyla.

"Look, it *is* your father. Lyshyla is with him as well." Oadira pointed. "What are they doing here? Did they know we were coming?"

"I'm sick of this," Ozias spat, stepping from behind the tree and walking purposefully toward his father and friend. "What are you doing here, Father?"

"I could ask the same of you and our Sahaelian guest," King Nilhist said, face emotionless.

Oadira walked quickly to keep up with Ozias, but she was nervous about what his apparent anger would mean to their quest for knowledge. It seemed the king had been more insightful about their time in the library than he had implied.

"I asked you about the Orishan bloodline and Sahael," Ozias said, finger pointing as he stomped up to the king. "I asked you for Oadira, and you wouldn't tell me anything."

“You weren’t ready for that knowledge, and neither is the princess,” Nilhist said with a glance toward Oadira. “Once my guards reported you two had gone missing yesterday evening, I knew where to come. We rode hard from that moment to make sure I arrived before you. There will be no entering this pyramid today or ever.”

“Why not?” she spat. Oadira had endured enough of this. Solomon had told her to come to Iceoth. She knew she could find answers here, and she wasn’t leaving without them.

“You don’t get to question me, child,” Nilhist said, face hard as granite. “I’ve lived more than a dozen of your lifetimes. I’ve kept my people safe all that time.”

“And will that safety continue, Father?” Ozias asked forcefully. “Not two hours ago, Oadira and I found water from the lake flowing east toward the ocean, not west toward the city. We also saw what looked like a force of Daleans amassing on the coast where the bay used to be too hazardous to land.”

King Nilhist didn’t seem shocked to hear about Dalean forces landing en masse inland. He took a few steps down toward Ozias. He glanced at Oadira, and his eyes shifted into a cold, dirty glare. The king turned his back to them and spoke with Lyshyla once more.

“Are you going to do anything about the threat of Dalean forces in Iceoth?” asked Ozias.

The king glanced at Oadira, ignoring his son’s question. “We will not engage with Dalean forces. That is precisely what they want from us. It would reveal our location. In addition, their attacks could wipe us out. We have remained safe and off their maps for years because we’ve chosen not to engage.”

“Of course,” Oadira sneered. “You just take the people coming to you for refuge and set them up in surrounding settlements to draw the Dale attacks and those innocent people die by their swords as your protective barrier."

"Such is the way of Iceoth," Nilhist said, turning back towards them with a slight smile.

Infuriated, Ozias stood nose-to-nose with his father. "So, you will do nothing? You would just let them die?"

"Yes," said King Nilhist. "And since when did that bother you, Prince of Iceoth? None of this has changed since the time of your arrival."

Ozias stuttered for a second, glancing at Oadira before continuing. "We're not talking about a few raiding parties, Father. We were twenty miles away, but I could tell there was a much larger force than usual amassing to the east. We're talking about letting people be completely wiped out. We have the Anubis guards here. We can use them to help defend the refugees. I've been working with these people from the colonies, getting to know them. They are stronger than we assumed. They have survived hardship, and that has made them strong, not weak like we thought. The warriors can help protect them, and the former slaves will fight. I know it now."

Nilhist stepped away from Ozias and looked directly at Oadira. "Ever since you arrived on Iceoth's coast, the seas, lakes, and rivers have changed. Their currents have reversed course. Can you explain this phenomenon?"

Oadira didn't respond. She was afraid if she opened her mouth, she would end up cursing the king, screaming at him for his arrogance and pride.

"Open your eyes," commanded the Nilhist. "The reversed currents have caused parts of the caverns to melt away. The waters that flowed west now flow east. The currents have brought unwanted ships and invaders to Iceoth's coasts." King Nilhist strode wearily back along the path, facing his army. The Ankh necklace of Anubis around his neck showed his authority and control of his military. "In direct response to what has transpired, these warriors will be used to defend Benin and Benin only." He turned to face his son and Oadira. "The refugees and the people in the surrounding cities will continue to be the buffer for Benin."

"So, you will just leave them out there defenseless?" Ozias asked.

"Yes," King Nilhist answered.

"We need to do something about this!" Odira cried, not caring what she said or who she said it to. "You allowed these people to come here, promised they would be safe if they worked the farms, and now you must do all that is within your power to protect them! That is what an honorable king would do."

Nilhist turned toward Oadira, eyes inflamed with rage.

Lyshyla stepped between Oadira and her monarch. "King Nilhist," she began slowly. "Perhaps we can send a small cohort to lead the people here to the caverns in a slightly forceful way. The plant and animal life here won't sustain a group so large for long, but it will get them out of harm's way. I feel that this will ensure that the refugees stay safe."

"Yes!" Ozias said, "Please, allow Oadira and I the responsibility of looking over them."

The king paused before speaking. "No!"

"If you send the Anubis warriors above, then we can get to the cities in time," Ozias said with a slightly lower tone, reflecting the command of a future king.

Educator Lyshyla stepped forward again. "I believe such a force will suffice. My king, it would be wise to heed the counsel of your son."

King Nilhist turned without a word, making his way up the stairs at the pyramid's entrance. "Educator Lyshyla, return my son and his companion to Benin where they will be under house arrest in the palace until further notice."

"Father," Ozias pleaded. "At least let Oadira and I inside the pyramid so she can learn how she can return to Sahael. She was told to come here by Solomon himself. At least give us that, please!"

"I need to learn about my people," Oadira demanded.

"You'll mind your tone," said the king. "Why is it so important you enter?"

Oadira grew reticent, knowing she needed to choose her words carefully.

"I am the last of my bloodline. The Orishan Bloodline."

"Are you the Orishan destined to usher in the Signs of the Times?" asked Lyshyla.

"That is what Solomon told me and my cousins, yes," replied Oadira. "You know all of this, I'm sure, King Nilhist. From the moment you saw my eyes and hair when I arrived, you've treated me like a snake about to strike."

As she spoke, blue Orishan tattoos started to glow on her arms and legs as proof of her words.

"King Nilhist," Lyshyla said, staring at Oadira's tattoos. "For thousands of years, the Ancient Bloodlines adorned their bodies with permanent symbols as a method of curing illness, providing protections, showing loyalty to their tribe, and denoting their social status. The ancients used tattoos to demonstrate specific personality traits of self-expression and storytelling. The Signs of the Times are truly upon us."

"And they will destroy us, if we let them," the king

whispered.

"You don't know that!" Oadira shouted.

"I know everything!" King Nilhist screamed, voice echoing through the massive cavern; face a contorted mass of fury. "Do you expect me to drop to one knee and bow in reverence before you? I am a king!"

A few birds squawked at the disturbance, but other than that, silence reigned. Nilhist breathed deeply through his flared nostrils. Oadira stood her ground.

"I never wanted to be a queen," Oadira said, voice quiet, eyes on her furry boots. "For my entire life that I can remember, I was pampered like a turkey being fattened for a feast so I could be bred out for the optimum price. All I wanted was to be free." She looked Nilhist in his eyes. "Now all I want is for my people to be free. For all people to be free. Whether it's my fault or not, your world is changing. I felt it in the water. You can do what you want. It's your kingdom. But let me do what I need to do. Let me into this pyramid so I can learn what Solomon sent me here to learn. You may think nothing but disaster can come from the Signs of the Times, but I don't think that's the case. Please, let me in. Let me learn what I need to learn about Sahael. Let me at least have a chance to save my people…to save *our* people."

Nilhist's breaths came slow and steady. The vein on his temple stopped throbbing.

"You may enter the pyramid and read the texts," he said slowly. "You may find what you need, or you may not, but I won't stand in your way."

"Thank you, your majesty." Oadira reached for Ozias's hand and started walking up the pyramid's stairs.

"I acknowledge your claim," King Nilhist said, holding up a hand. "But my son is to stay here with me." King Nilhist stepped closer to Oadira and stared her down with his piercing eyes. "Lyshyla can go with you. She knows the lore as well as anyone on Iceoth. You might have the Chosen Blood or the Ancient Blood, but let me be clear, you have no power over me. You cannot control my people, and that remains true for my son, Prince Ozias Ocnus."

"Please, can't he come with me?" asked Oadira with a look of frustration wrinkling her brow. "We traveled here together. We worked together."

"You, Oadira," said King Nilhist with a voice tainted in malice, "are a queen to a people that no longer exists. You are the last of the Orishas, a people rumored to have been systematically exterminated from the face of Aarde by Lord Commander Natas himself. Only tiny remnants of your people remain, but they have chosen exile, hiding all over Aarde, in Iceoth, the outer provinces, and Sahaedron."

"The gathering made it possible," Lyshyla interjected.

"I don't understand," Oadira said.

"The gathering of Watchers and those on the Nibiru wall connected to the Ancient Bloodlines in Sahael," Lyshyla said. "As an Educator, I know the lore and history. It was a decree handed down by Ishtar and Obatala to the Watchers, Sahaelians, Horn, and the Egyptians to submit their loyalty and lives to Sahael, making them the Chosen Bloodlines of the people. Your bloodline was created to serve and protect the people of Alkebulan. You obviously failed. The Orishan bloodline, the Hausan bloodline, the Yoruban bloodline, and the Demirrian bloodline are the four new lineages that came out of those unions. That is why you have no power here. We are not of your bloodline or people. Not anymore. King Nilhist has spoken."

"As I said," replied King Nilhist, whose voice cast a pall over everyone who heard it, "you have no authority here."

Ozias' teeth clenched tightly. He squeezed Oadira's hand and then let go. He looked at Lyshyla. "Fine. I'll stay here. But the army needs to be mobilized."

"Absolutely not," King Nilhist interrupted. "My army will remain hidden in the caverns as they have for the last decade. If needed, they will defend Benin. For now, they will guard the pyramid. Ozias will go to the surface with me."

All Oadira could do was remain steadfast in her pursuit of answers. Lyshyla stayed with Oadira as Ozias disappeared entirely from view with his father as they walked back through the trees.

"Are you sure you want answers?" Lyshyla asked. "You may not like them."

"I have nothing to fear from the truth," Oadira said with a joyless smile. "You may, but I don't. Let's go."

CHAPTER V

THE ARCHIVES OF ICEOTH

Iceoth Caverns, Iceoth

Inside the ice-stone pyramid of Iceoth, stood an immense open space in the same triangular shape as the exterior structure; a square base with four sides meeting at a point far overhead. Large round stones set into the walls glowed pale blue, not unlike the cavern itself. Darkness dispelled, Oadira looked at what appeared to be infinite rows of books, scrolls, and loose papers. The main level housed a majority of the Anubis warriors, who had followed them inside. Dust covered everything within. The smell of mold and rotting paper permeated the room. Small rodents, such as snow rats and snow mice, scurried across the floors, squeaks echoing against the stone all around.

Oadira, still distraught over the experience with King Nilhist, could remain silent no longer. "Who does he think he is?" she said wildly.

Lyshyla turned to Oadira, "He is the king. His word is law, and he rules with an iron fist. As he prepares to protect his people, every man, woman, and child, from the threat of invasion, he believes your presence endangers them all."

Oadira lowered her head in anger, but Lyshyla lifted her chin.

"But I know why you have come," said Lyshyla. "Solomon sent you. He knew that the concealing power of Nebiriau's bracelet would soon fade, exposing your sapphire eyes permanently. That is the reason he ordered you here. To usher in the Signs of the Times. It started with the rebellions awakening the Diaspora, allowing you the chance to escape here, to Iceoth. You are a force for good."

"Then why didn't you say anything?" Oadira asked.

"Who am I to tell Nilhist otherwise? I need to stay in the king's good graces to ensure that I will continue to have access to these historical records."

"What is your true purpose for being here?" Oadira asked. "You're an educator, right? You learn and know things. You're supposed to teach others the truth."

Lyshyla looked around as if making sure no one was in earshot of her subsequent response.

"You, the lost pharaoh," she began, "and the Nairohenge Gates of Aarde are my purposes for being here. You are right. I am an Educator, working on becoming a Professor. My purpose is to help you and Ozias in any way that I can."

"Okay," Odira said, running her fingers along the edge of a large leatherbound book on a shelf. "Solomon mentioned these gates allow people to travel between different places through portals, right? I know I need to find one, and I thought there might be one on Iceoth, but all the documents he gave me were destroyed in a fire during the rebellion and escape. I don't know what to look for, and I don't have enough history of my people to make any intelligent decisions. Can you help me find the gates and learn more about my bloodline?"

Lyshyla agreed to the proposition with a single nod.

“Let’s get started. It will take my mind off Ozias.” Oadira sighed a heavy sigh. “I wish he were here with me.”

“Do you love him?” Lyshyla asked.

“I don’t even know what love is,” Oadira responded honestly.

“Well, in my experience,” Lyshyla started, “love is when you cannot breathe around that person. It’s when you take stock of all the people and things this world has to offer, and all of it pales in comparison to a single moment with them. Those moments let you know when someone is your soulmate. I have seen the way you two look at each other. It’s obvious you both love each other deeply.”

Oadira pondered her thoughts on love. She started with her mother and father. Though she barely remembered her time with them, she’d never forgotten their sacrifices. Her mind shifted to Amahlé, who raised her and always held her best interest at heart. Those connections shaped her, filling her with a deep need to love and be loved. The attachment she developed with Prince Ozias gave her feelings of breathlessness, and when he was around, everything paled in comparison. She felt love for the prince, and love had to be what he felt for her in return. They had walked together across Iceoth facing freezing temperatures and danger, and yet even when running from the spiders, Oadira knew Ozias would protect her at all costs.

Lyshyla shrugged nonchalantly. “It won’t matter whether the two of you are in love or not. King Nilhist will make sure that you are never united in any meaningful way.”

“Why?” asked Oadira. Lyshyla’s statement hadn’t been surprising, but she wanted more insights into why the king was so intent on not letting them get too close.

“King Nilhist knows that if you marry Ozias, he will

become the new king by the Chosen Right of Election," Lyshyla explained.

"What is the Chosen Right of Election?" Oadira asked.

Lyshyla strode deeper into the library and beckoned Oadira forward. Oadira followed, observing the thousands of library books stacked in limitless rows.

"What is the Chosen Right of Election?" Oadira inquired again.

Lyshyla stopped at a bookshelf and pulled out an old scroll rolled up with a piece of leather tied in a knot. She unpicked the tie and opened the scroll, which was written in a script Oadira couldn't read.

"The Chosen Right of Election," Lyshyla began, "is the right placed upon the queens of the Chosen Bloodline. When one marries into the lineage of the Ancient Bloodline, they become of the same bloodline, inheriting her ideal traits such as her eye color and extended immortality. Ozias' right to the throne will supersede his father's." Lyshyla turned from the scroll and made eye contact with Oadira. Her expression and tone grew stern. "You need to be careful."

Perplexed, Oadira said, "Tell me why."

"King Nilhist is aware of the love between you two. And because of this, he will marry off his son as soon as possible," Lyshyla said. "To someone else."

"Why is that such a big deal?" Oadira inquired.

"When that happens, the Chosen Right of Election becomes null and void," Lyshyla said, shaking her head in frustration. "King Nilhist won't have to worry about losing his power and his right to rule. The moment he realized the two of you had left the city yesterday evening and were likely coming here, he called in one of his regents to begin the process of betrothal and consummation."

“This is all happening so fast. What are you saying to me?” Oadira asked.

Lyshyla placed her hand on Oadira’s shoulder. “Do you know what you are?”

“Only what Solomon has told me,” said Oadira.

“Oadira, you are one of the four Black Madonnas.”

“I don’t know what that means!” Oadira shouted, voice echoing through the cavernous room. She dropped her voice, looking around as if waiting for one of the soldiers of Anubis to rush over and arrest her for yelling. “I recall Solomon mentioning that, but he didn’t go into any detail at the time. What more can you tell me about the Black Madonnas?”

“The right of the Black Madonna is one in which pure virgins would emerge from the four Kemettian bloodlines and the four Chosen Bloodlines. When the two pedigrees merged, they created the Ancient Bloodlines, and a Black Madonna from each of the four lineages emerged from it,” Lyshyla explained.

“The other princesses and I are tasked with getting back to Sahael,” Odira said. “What purpose do the Black Madonnas play within the four bloodlines?”

“You have it written all over your body,” Lyshyla said, motioning toward Oadira’s arms. “Your tattoos tell the story in ancient script and symbol. ‘From their wombs, savior kings will come forth uniting and saving the Sahaelian and Alkebulan people from enslavement and captivity to the witan nations on Aarde.’”

Oadira was in complete shock hearing these words out of Lyshyla’s mouth. She remembered reading something along those lines regarding the birth of kings in Solomon’s documents, but it hadn’t meant anything to her. Now she understood what he had meant by things not making sense until she had arrived in Iceoth.

Lyshyla touched Oadira’s shoulder softly. “All four of you,

your sister-cousins, must find a way to marry the proper person. If you don't, your bloodlines will no longer have the combined powers you share equally, thus making you a tribeless queen."

Everything made sense now. Solomon had sent her here not to find merely some hidden gate, but to discover the man who would help her merge the bloodlines. Ozias' eyes had turned blue in the sacred waters of Oth-Lake. He had hidden tattoos as well.

Ozias was her chosen mate.

Her stomach flittered at the thought. Perhaps this was what love felt like. She liked it.

"Is there anything that can be done?" Oadira asked.

Lyshyla grinned and nodded her head down the row of books and documents. "Yes, we will have to use the old ways to make it happen."

Lyshyla grabbed Oadira's hand, and the two women ran down row after row of books. Stopping in front of a grouping of two shelves flanking a statue of the symbol of Horus, a pyramid with a stylized eye engraved in gold, Lyshyla grabbed a book that seemed slightly smaller than all the others.

"This is a Nalace journal given to Educators," Lyshyla said, handing the book to Oadira. "It is an item of great knowledge and power. It has unlimited pages allowing educators such as myself to write down all that they see. The information is sent to the library of Timbuktu, where the Masters in Timbuktu decipher the information making it digestible for the learning, researching, and lecturing of the chosen teachers. Professor Nalace created the journals allowing the Educators and Timbuktu to capture all the secrets inside and outside of Aarde."

"What do you want me to do with this?" Oadira asked.

"You asked if anything could be done. This Nalace journal will provide you with some answers," Lyshyla said. "It is a compendium of everything written by educators across the world. Come. There is a sitting area where you can read."

Near the center of the open space inside the pyramid, Lyshyla led Oadira to an area with large pillows and small tables where visitors could lounge and read. Orbs of yellow light floated above, casting the area in a warm and comfortable glow.

"Sit here, read," Lyshyla said, motioning for Oadira to make herself comfortable. "I'll get us some food from the soldier's kitchen tent. Read, and you can ask me questions once you're ready."

Oadira sat among the soft cushions as Lyshyla wandered back through the maze of bookshelves. She opened the Nalace journal and started to read, finding her fingers gravitate toward the pages with the information she sought. Nygaard's prophecy about a virgin that would come to Iceoth's shores caught her eye, as did the writing of an unnamed educator that spoke of watching over a princess in a plantation house preparing for rebellion.

Lyshyla returned with food, but would wander off, allowing Oadira to read alone for hours on end before checking on her to make sure she didn't need anything or have any questions.

"The rights, privileges, and gifts that the Orishan bloodlines offer are to benefit their chosen offspring, who are to carry their lineage forward for future generations," Oadira read out loud, finding the words powerful and strangely soothing. *"A queen within any of the Chosen Bloodlines will supersede any king within their respective Sahaelian bloodline. The prince, the son of the king, assumes the title of king, and the wife assumes the title of queen. The former king and queen become stewards of the chosen and Ancient Bloodline."*

King Nilhist's worry of losing his throne came into stark focus. Was this the reason he never wanted Ozias to read from the books here in the archive? Her distaste for the long-lived king grew with each passage. Apparently living for over 300 years didn't remove an individual's penchant for selfishness and need for power over others.

Lyshyla returned once more with another platter of food.

"Night has fallen outside the caverns," she said, placing the food on a short table beside Oadira. "You can continue reading, but I would suggest you take some rest as well. Princess of Sahael or not, you must be tired after trekking all last night and a good portion of the day to get here."

"This is dangerous information," Oadira said, tapping her finger against the passage she had just read.

"What are you going to do about it?" Lyshyla asked.

"I say we use it," Oadira said confidently. "You told me King Nilhist plans to marry off Ozias in order to keep his throne. These laws are more powerful than the king's petty desires."

"I agree," replied Lyshyla. "But using this information will not be as easy as you think."

"I didn't say it would be easy," Oadira said.

"Don't jump off the cliff until you know you can survive the fall," Lyshyla said with a smile. "It's an old saying we have here in Iceoth. I serve the king, but I know the Signs of the Times as well. For now, we will keep any plans to ourselves until the time is right. When that time comes, we will use it to benefit you and Ozias. You can count on my support."

"This information will be hard for many people in the kingdom to accept," said Oadira.

"Yes," nodded Lyshyla. "Especially the king, who will have to humble himself immensely to accept such terms."

"This is a lot to take in," said Oadira. "These laws are ancient. How are we to force others to uphold them?"

Lyshyla turned away from her. "There is no way to know how people will react. I'm sure during your escape from the colonies you saw slaves helping their masters to quell the riots, actively participating in their own oppression. All we can do is trust in the foresight of the gods and pray our actions ignite a fire within them."

"I know what I must do," said Oadira finally. "But if I am to make it happen, I'll need your help."

Lyshyla paused for a moment, bowing her head. "I told you I am at yours' and Ozias' service. I will do it for the Bloodline. The best thing you can do is take this process step by step. I'll assist you along the way. Did you find anything on Nabtahenge or any of the other gateways?"

"I've been looking for any clues to help me get back home to Sahael. There is so much here to read, I'm unsure where to go next."

"You'll find what you search for," Lyshyla said as she took a bite of an orange fruit from the platter. "The book has a way of helping you find the answers most pressing in your mind. It's a helpful magic that goes back to Timbuktu. You'll find it. Search some of the other books as well. We have tomes of history and art, things that will ignite memories that belonged to your ancestors but remain in your lineage. Remember, knowledge is kept within your bloodline. Whatever you read, you will have the ability to remember and pass it down to your offspring. In your case, this is why you have to get to Sahael, because all your knowledge will return to the forefront of your mind when the first gathering is complete."

"Solomon said something similar to that when he first revealed everything to my sisters and I," Oadira mentioned.

Oadira strolled down the aisle of the massive library. Overwhelmed by the vast ocean of literature, Oadira's hesitation turned into frustration.

"Where do I look? Half the books aren't even written in a language I can read."

"Just give it time," Lyshyla said, eating more fruit and chewing slowly. "Start with the history of your people. As you read, you will develop an uncanny ability to understand more than you could ever imagine. Simply close your eyes and pick a book. Let your ancestors guide you now. Trust in their wisdom. And as a princess of Sahael, I would assume you will soon realize you can read very quickly and retain the knowledge. It is part of your bloodline. Ozias has this same gift. Use it."

Oadira took a deep breath, releasing the frustration clouding her senses. She ran her eyes across the leather spines and came upon one that emanated bright blue. Gold lettering on the binding read *The Ancient Blood of the Orisha*. She grabbed the book from the shelf, opened the front cover, and began reading.

The words of Solomon came to her mind as she read about Nyathera's asteroid and a group of ancient Kemites that left the planet Kolob after starting and finishing a civil war. They used the civil war as a distraction to commandeer Nyathera's last operational ship, which was designed as a large rock broke into multiple pieces as it entered Aarde's atmosphere, hitting different continents in Aarde.

Oadira slept at times but had no idea when the sun was up outside the caverns and when it was night. All that existed were the books and the knowledge they contained. She read books about the Ukávááł, who destroyed their planet of Kolob and ushered in a sentient, experiential, and humanoid army. She read about the kingdom of Egyptus, the four lost pharaohs, and the three empires in Alkebulan. She repeatedly spoke to herself about what she had learned. Lyshyla would answer questions now and then, but for the most part, Oadira was content to read and absorb.

"I never knew being educated could open my mind to things the witans were afraid of people like me knowing," Oadira said to herself as Lyshyla listened.

Eventually, after several days, the guards of Anubis spoke with Lyshyla, informing her the king had terminated their access to the pyramid, and they would return that day to Benin by way of horse-drawn sled. Disappointment clawed at Oadira's heart, but she was also excited to see Ozias again. The handful of days they'd been apart had begun to fill her heart with longing.

During their trek under the sun in the cold Iceoth air, Oadira and Lyshyla rode in the sled side-by-side, speaking about the future and how they might bring about the best outcome for all peoples.

"I sent a message to Ozias two days ago with one of the king's servants who came to check on us," Lyshyla said as the sled hit a rock and bounced a bit. "He replied and it's been agreed that in the morning, he'll meet you outside the city, beneath the grove of Marula Trees in full bloom. I've created a large window of time for the two of you where the king will be unaware you are together. I have to relocate the outer city guards to the perimeter of the pyramid, but it will be worth it."

That evening Oadira and Lyshyla arrived in Benin and were escorted to their quarters. Oadira's were exactly as she had left them the night she and Ozias made their clandestine trek to the archives. She slept fitfully, thinking of Ozias' face, and the thought that the king was planning his marriage to someone else at that very moment.

"It's been a while since we've last seen each other," Ozias said, unable to shift his sight from Oadira as they sat alone beneath the Marula tree.

"I'm sorry,' said Oadira, who grinned and shyly averted her gaze. "Lyshyla kept me pretty busy reading book after book in the archive. I found that the longer I focused, the faster I read. It was pretty amazing. I was getting through some books in a matter of minutes by the last day."

"How many can you read in an hour?" Ozias asked, eyes wide.

"Twelve," Oadira giggled.

"That is wonderful. Keep up the good work," said Ozias with a grin.

"Lyshyla mentioned that you have the gift as well and that you can read a lot of books. How many could you read in an hour?" Oadira asked.

"Twenty-six," Ozias said.

Oadira's mouth dropped open. "Forgive me for asking."

"You wanted to know," he said playfully with a smirk. Ozias touched her hand, sending a shiver down her spine.

"I have heard some rumors about you," she said nervously.

"What rumors?" Ozias said.

"Just rumors," said Oadira, twisting a blue braid in her hair.

"There are always rumors going around the city about me.

Tell me, what you have you heard this time?" Ozias asked with seriousness on his face.

"I heard from Lyshyla that you're going to be married soon and that King Nilhist is the one arranging it," Oadira said. The words sparked a sadness in Oadira, causing sapphire tears to run slowly down her ebony cheeks. "I'm sorry it bothers me, but it does. He's going to force you to marry someone…else."

Ozias wrapped his arms around her and held her as tight and close as possible.

"That's not true," he said. "I'm not sure what my father has planned or what's going on. But trust me when I say that I'll find out as soon as I can. This all seems like a sick mind game my father is playing with you. I promise you I'll get to the bottom and let you know what I find out."

Oadira broke from his embrace. "It's getting late," she said. "Your father will wonder where you've run off to."

"You're right, but a little while longer won't hurt. I miss being in your presence and feeling your lips pressed against mine," Ozias smiled. "I keep thinking about floating underwater and having you breathe for me. It was a…unique experience."

"It's not worth the risk of upsetting your father and having to do something even more irrational than running off to the archives," Oadira cautioned.

"Okay, but as soon as I find out what is going on, I'll contact you. I promise." Ozias leaned forward quickly, and his lips met Oadira's. She could do nothing but melt in his embrace. After parting, they headed in separate directions, back to their quarters.

That evening, an hour before dinner, guards arrived at Oadira's chambers with an invitation to dine with the royal court in the palace. The way the guards stood there at attention, Oadira inferred it was not a request. She followed her escorts to the palace where she was once again taken into the dining hall with its tall arched ceilings and crystalline stone walls. She was seated at the far end of a long table, like a person who needed to know they were not as important as they thought they were. Twenty other royal guests crowded the banquet board, each trying to scooch closer to the king as if the mere proximity to him would give them power.

During dinner, King Nilhist stood smiling and held up a silver goblet.

"Today is a special occasion," King Nilhist said. "Which is why you have all been invited here. Some of you may have heard rumors lately---"

"Rumors of a secret marriage involving me," Prince Ozias interrupted, causing his father to stumble on his words.

"…Yes, I have arranged a secret marriage for you," King Nilhist said, face no longer pleasant and friendly. "This is a joyous occasion, so please, treat your king and your future wife with respect. May I introduce Princess Onissa of the Snow Canyon People of Iceoth."

A woman sitting across from Ozias stood and bowed as party patrons clapped politely, oohing and awing.

Princess Onissa stood six-feet, five-inches tall with long, jet-black, straight hair, ivory teeth, and long slender legs and a well-proportioned frame. She had light, bluish-white eyes that matched her majestic smile. Oadira couldn't say she disliked the woman, never having met her before, but something about the princess made Oadira pretty sure she wouldn't like her.

"May I also introduce her mother, Ova," King Nilhist continued. "Her father, Olit, and their royal guard."

The man and woman seated next to Onissa stood and bowed as well. They both looked appropriately royal with fine robes and gold accents. Again, the dinner guests fawned over them and applauded sycophantically.

"A secret marriage? Why are you telling me this now?" Prince Ozias asked, tossing his fork onto his plate and standing next to his father. "I'm not marrying anybody!"

"Yes, you are!" King Nilhist said, voice growing louder. The clapping stopped, many of the guests staring intently at their plates. "You will do as your king commands! Do I make myself clear?"

"Why are you doing this?" Prince Ozias asked.

Nilhist glanced quickly at Oadira but returned his gaze to Ozias almost instantly. "To protect you, the people, and Iceoth."

"To protect yourself!" Ozias shouted before turning from the table and stomping out the door.

Had Lyshyla told him about the Chosen Right of Election? Did he know about what would happen if he married Oadira?

The dinner continued in silence after that. Oadira wanted to get up and leave too but figured it would only make matters worse if she ran off to Ozias in the presence of the court. She didn't need to give King Nilhist any more reason to think she was a threat to his reign.

As one of the servers was taking Oadira's empty plate between the main course and their sweet pudding dessert, she felt a piece of paper slide into her hand as it lay on the table. Without looking up at the attendant as they walked back toward the kitchens, Oadira quickly hid the paper on her lap. As dinner concluded and everyone was gushing about the meal and the news of Ozias' imminent wedding, Oadira walked over to the pillars on the far side of the hall and read the note.

It was from Ozias.

Meet me as soon as possible at our favorite spot.

"What did he write?"

Oadira jumped when she heard the voice, but her heart steadied when she saw Lyshyla sidle next to her behind the pillar.

"You scared me!" Oadira hissed. She handed Lyshyla the note.

"This is real," Lyshyla said. "It's Ozias' handwriting."

"Should I go? At this point, the king is going to be watching every move I make in the city. He seemed to know Ozias and I had feelings for each other before we even did."

"We all saw your attraction before the two of you did," Lyshyla mused. She glanced from behind the pillar at the group still talking in the hall. "Go. Ozias knows his father will be watching. If he's called you to see him, it's for a reason. Trust him. He seems to be more thoughtful since your arrival in Benin; less brash. You've been a good influence on him."

Oadira left the banquet, bowing to members of the court and thanking the king for his invitation. She even smiled at Onissa and congratulated her. Once outside, Oadira made her way to the city walls and stood alone on the ice surrounded by Marula Trees, waiting for Ozias to show his face.

She heard a whisper. Oadira turned and headed toward the sound and found Ozias peeking through the branches of a berry bush. It was dark, but her bright-blue eyes allowed her to see him clearly.

"You are being watched," he said. "Keep your eyes front and center. Pretend to be picking some berries."

Oadira turned away from him, and to any soul watching, she appeared completely alone. Whomever the king had watching her was very good at hiding their presence. She began picking berries and chewing them slowly.

"I know my father has increased security in the city and on the outskirts," Ozias said. "I am to marry a young woman I have never seen or met. But I refused to go through with it."

"Nonsense! You must go through with it," Oadira whispered.

Leaves on the bush rustled as if Ozias was unhappy with that comment. "Why?"

"If you don't, a civil war will break out," Oadira said. "Lyshyla and I talked about this quite a bit while at the pyramid together. It will destroy everything you and your father built and could destroy his bloodline and mine from within."

"Then what do you suggest we do?" Ozias asked. "I don't want to marry her. I want to marry…I just don't want to marry her."

"Lyshyla and I have come up with a plan. Just go along with the wedding. It will all work out," Oadira assured. "You need to trust me."

"What's the plan?"

"I don't have time to tell you all about it because if I did, the plan would not work," said Oadira. "You must have deniability just in case something goes wrong. Tell your father you'll marry Onissa willingly and without a shouting match. Tell him you know it's for the good of the kingdom and you will follow his wishes. Again, please trust me."

"I do." a hand reached out from the bush and grabbed Oadira's as she picked another berry. "Oadira I…I just want you to know that I've truly appreciated our time together. I know that when we first met, I was childish and rude, but I hope that since then…I mean…I've tried to…I just…"

The bush rustled again, and Ozias stood tall, out in the open for everyone to see. He touched Oadira's face and then kissed her passionately. A warmth spread through her body, and she found herself drawing closer to Ozias, as if trying to pull them together into one person.

Guards shouted in the distance. They had come looking for Ozias and a stolen kiss had given them his location.

"Go!" Oadira ordered. "Trust me!"

"I will." Ozias turned and started running under the adjacent Marula trees. A giant grin spread across his face as he turned back to look at her. "I love you, Oadira! I love you!"

"I love you too," Oadira smiled.

Ozias hurried off. Movement along the walls and in the garden told Oadira that the guards were following their crown prince. What would King Nilhist do when he found out they had kissed in the garden? Hopefully Ozias would tell him it was their last kiss goodbye and that he would marry Onissa willingly. If he did that, their plan could work.

It had to work.

He's mine, and I'm going to do everything in my power to keep it that way, Oadira said internally.

CHAPTER VI

THE MARRIAGE COVENANT

Iceoth, Benin City, Capital Palace

In the year 1519 of the Iceoth and grander Alkebulan calendar, Aarde's Equinox brought with it not only pinnacle of the sun's movement from the south to the north, but Prince Ozias's wedding as well. The florists, chefs, and bards performed their duties, and the wedding officiant prepared. At the request of King Nilhist, representatives from the great lineages across Iceoth came to pay their respects.

Oadira watched the festivities with a mixture of amusement and fear. Ozias was her chosen mate. Of that she had no doubt. If Solomon were here, she knew he would confirm her promptings. Even so, the crown prince was marrying someone else. For weeks now, Oadira and Lyshyla had finalized their plans, hoping everything would work out the way they wanted.

And now the day of truth had arrived.

The dancers performed tribally choreographed prances throughout the capital city of Benin, showing respect and reverence to the royal house. Streamers of icicles hung from balconies and across bridges. Even on the warmest day of the year, frost still clung to rooftops. The cold bothered no one though, as the festivities continued throughout the day. Wrestlers readied themselves for matches, a custom of the culture that reminded Oadira of the Royal Rumble. The people enjoyed exquisite food and wine. Carolers wandered the streets singing tribal songs of triumph and love.

Outside the royal palace, Oadira waited for Lyshyla. Revelers danced and sang all around, but Oadira felt only the twisting of her nervous stomach.

"It's time," Lyshyla whispered in Oadira's ear, making her jump.

Turning, Oadira saw Lyshyla, a woman who had become her friend over the preceding months, dressed in a colorful dress with white Iceoth symbols sewn into the patterns. She grabbed Oadira's arm and rushed her through several servant hallways and eventually to a room adjacent to the ceremonial hall.

"We need to hurry," Lyshyla said, closing the door behind her. She ran to a wardrobe on the far wall and pulled out a royal Miriam cape gown with sapphire trim. Oadira gasped at its beauty.

"Where's Onissa?" Oadira asked as she took the dress from Lyshyla.

"Exactly where she's supposed to be: unconscious in one of the servant rooms," Lyshyla smiled. "I made sure she had plenty to drink all night and into this morning. Ozias' chief servant Ossa kept the Amarula flowing. Onissa had no problem accepting his gifts of liquor. That woman talked a lot once she got fired up with wine. She would be no good for Ozias. Her only desire is to marry and have kids and have no opinions of her own. Such things are, 'unbecoming a servant queen,' she said. Ozias needs an equal, not a sex slave. You wouldn't imagine the things she asked me about how to please Ozias sexually. She certainly wanted to make him happy."

“I’m sure she did.” Oadira finished putting on the dress and Lyshyla helped with the buttons.

“And you made sure to shape-change to look like her when you made it through the gates, right?” Lyshyla asked, fingers buttoning as fast as they could. “We don’t want anyone to know she didn’t make it to the morning check-in.”

“I was there, and I looked like her, as planned,” Oadira confirmed. “Then I turned back into myself so that I could check in as well. I know King Nilhist wants to rub the ceremony in my face, and I’d hate for him to think I was less than gracious.”

Oadira looked at her reflection in a full-figure mirror in the corner. She looked like a beautiful bride ready to be united with her love.

“Put on the veil,” Lyshyla said. “It’s tradition for the groom to not see his bride’s face. You could choose to skin-change into Onissa again, but I know you want to marry Ozias as yourself, which I agree with. Ozias loves you and you love him. I am excited to unite the two of you. Let’s go!”

The halls were full of people as Lyshyla led Oadira to the altar where she and Ozias would be married. The whole city gathered, happy to be part of the festivities. As the wedding festivities commenced, Prince Ozias entered the hall with his head held high. He looked truly regal in his wedding garb, a lovely white dashiki, Ankara pants with blue trim, white shoes, and a fitted white hat featuring the symbol of Ankh. The prince’s entourage consisted of his bodyguards, ring boys, groomsmen, his father’s closest friends, and his best friend, Ossa, accompanying him at the far end of the great chamber.

“Prince Ozias Ocnus!” shouted the crier to the cheer of thousands of excited guests. Oadira wanted to rush toward Ozias and kiss him, but stayed silent and unmoving so as not to make anyone think she was anything but docile Princess Onissa.

The crowd silenced as the rhythmic beating of drums thumped around them. Lyshyla then walked down the aisle. She made eye contact with Prince Ozias, who was doing his best to be on his best behavior and not embarrass himself and his father.

Lyshyla stood at the head of the altar and motioned for Ozias to step toward his bride.

"May I present this Princess of Sahael," Lyshyla shouted. "She is worthy of our bloodline and the praise of our ancestors."

As the banjo's played, Ozias descended the aisle. He reached the altar and stopped next to Oadira. Lyshyla stood between them as the officiant of the ceremony. King Nilhist stood to Ozias's left. He smiled and nodded at Oadira.

What would you do if you knew I was under this veil? Oadira thought. *What will you do when you find out your plot has been thwarted? By the time you do, it will all be too late.*

Lyshyla began to officiate.

"Brothers and sisters, we stand here today under the eternal eyes of Ishtar and Obatala to wed the two strongest members of their bloodline. Merging these two souls to continue the legacy of their lineage is to bear a new generation of strong descent to bring about the first gathering of the twelve bloodlines."

The king coughed loudly, triggering Lyshyla to hurry and skip over the slow, dragging parts.

Lyshyla nodded.

Ozias scoffed at his father's impatience and desire to marry him off as quickly as possible. Even so, much to Oadira's relief, he remained silent as promised and allowed the ceremony to continue.

"Do you, Ozias Ocnus, vow to bring pride to your ancestors and descendants, through marriage with your bride, every day and every moment for eternity?" Lyshyla asked.

Ozias and the bride made eye contact.

Prince Ozias sighed. "I do," he said solemnly.

Lyshyla then turned to the bride. "Do you vow to bring pride to your ancestors and descendants, through marriage with your groom, as long as you both shall live?"

"I do," Oadira said quietly.

Lyshyla smiled. "By the power vested through the divine plan manifested by Ishtar and Obatala, I now pronounce you husband and wife. You are now bonded by mind, boy, and soul for eternity!"

The ring-bearers left with the rings to place them in the couple's new chambers, to be worn only after their consummation.

"The rings in which the two of you will swear fidelity, loyalty, and devotion to each other have been placed in your new chambers," Lyshyla said. "The flower girls have placed Snow Canyon poppies on the ground, and you are to lead your bride to your new chambers. A feast will be held this evening for the new bride and groom."

After Lyshyla finished officiating, the prince and princess were quickly escorted by the king's royal guards to the bridal quarters to consummate their marriage.

Ozias mumbled something about how his father couldn't hold the feast first, as was tradition, but wanted them to mate quickly so the whole thing could be over and done with. His frustration was evident.

The moment they entered the bridal suite, four awaiting maidservants rushed to the bride and started helping her remove her clothing. Two additional maidservants grabbed Prince Ozias by his hands and dragged him into the man's chamber to wash. The maids escorted the bride to the woman's section to prepare and bathe, never removing her veil, as that was the role of the new husband. Once the couple was fully prepped, the servants exited the room and closed the doors behind them.

Oadira stood by the bed wearing the veil and a sheer robe hanging loosely from her body.

Ozias approached, stepping into the room slowly, keeping his eyes on the floor.

"As is custom, I am to remove your veil, my love," Prince Ozias said.

He slowly and gently drew nearer to her and peered through the veil. But quickly, he averted his gaze, as his hands shook.

"I don't know if I can do this," he said. "I know, princess, we're married now, but I just need a minute…"

Oadira lifted the veil and smiled. Her hands returned to her side, and Ozias met her gaze once more.

Mouth agape, Ozias began to speak, but Oadira's hand leaped to his mouth, preventing him from making any noise.

"It's okay," she whispered. "I told you to trust Lyshyla and me." Oadira removed her hand from Ozias' mouth.

"How is this even possible?" Ozias asked, face alight with excitement.

"I have the ability to shape-shift and skin change," Odira began. She took his hand and kissed his knuckles. "Lyshyla tricked the bride into meeting last night and drinking a bit too much wine. The bride was so eager to learn how to please her future husband that she dared not pass up the opportunity. She disobeyed all protocol, making sure her personal guards couldn't track her movements at all, and consuming far too much liquor. From there, Lyshyla and Ossa left her in one of the servant bedrooms. I then shape-shifted to look like Onissa for the check-ins, and Lyshyla got me into the bridal dressing room. And here we are, married."

"The two of you did this all by yourself?" Ozias asked.

"No. Like I said, Ossa helped," Oadira said.

"Ossa!" Ozias laughed. "There has never been a better servant and best friend than that man." He grabbed Oadira and kissed her, picking her up and spinning around. "We're married!" he shouted as he put Oadira back down.

"Well," she began, tugging on the strap of her gown. "Technically we aren't married officially yet. Our bloodlines can't merge until we are one."

Oadira began to remove her sandals as she sat down on the bed. She slowly began to remove her gown.

"I love you," Ozias breathed.

"It's only a matter of time before your father starts pounding on our door," said an eager Oadira. She stood, wearing nothing but underwear and a sash covering her large breasts.

"I need to see the ring finger on your left hand," said Oadira.

Obeying the request, Ozias lifted his hand. Oadira removed one of Njiru's sapphire rings from her index finger and placed it on Ozias's ring finger.

"I am yours, and you are mine, for all eternity," Oadira said.

"I am yours, and you are mine, for all time and eternity," Ozias repeated.

Ozias slid onto the silk sheets and laid on his back.

"What do I do?" Oadira asked.

Ozias put his arms out, welcoming Oadira. "We'll figure it out together."

Oadira nervously crept into his arms as Ozias playfully brought her into his chest. He smiled at her and playfully tugged at her bottom lip.

Oadira returned the gesture, biting Ozias's top lip. He lifted into a sitting position and removed Oadira's sash as she unbuttoned and removed his dashiki. Ozias shimmied from his trousers. Oadira removed her underwear.

On their knees, they faced each other and kissed.

I love you, Oadira heard Ozias say. *I love you, Oadira. I love you.*

I love you too, she replied.

Only then did she realize they weren't speaking. Their minds had linked in that moment, just like Oadira's mind had linked with her cousins since childhood. Only pure love could do such a thing.

They looked at each other, as intimate as two people could be, bodies and minds merging.

Ozias smiled and kissed her again. *I love you, Oadira. For now, and always.*

I love you, Ozias. May we never be parted so long as our minds are intertwined.

Soon, their passion sent them into a loving embrace and their bodies intertwined like cobras, tussling across the bed.

CHAPTER VII

THE CHOSEN BLOODLINE

Iceoth, Benin City, Royal Chambers

After consummating their union, Oadira and Ozias truly became one. The tattoos on Prince Ozias began to light up a vivid cerulean color, as did his eyes. The power Oadira held within her bloodline unlocked what was inside Ozias as Ozias inserted himself inside Oadira.

After several hours, they exercised their newfound abilities and spoke through their shared minds. Now that they were one, their thoughts were linked eternally to each other for the benefit of their bloodline and people.

Oadira lay there in the crook of Ozias' arm, happier than she had ever been. All her life the thought of being bred out to the highest bidder, seeing the women of the plantation used and abused, taught Oadira that physical contact was a weapon, not a pleasure. But now she understood what love and safety truly were, what it meant to mutually surrender to each other, and that realization made their love transcendent and beautiful. She wept for all those who had never known a moment like this.

"What do we do from here?" Oadira asked as Ozias took a

deep breath and pulled her closer.

"At this point, I don't really care," Ozias replied.

"We do need to come up with something," Oadira said. "We'll be expected at the feast in an hour."

"Let's just enjoy our time together," Ozias said. "They can have the feast without us. If my father wanted to hold to tradition, he would have held the feast before ushering us off to consummate. If he can do that, I can forgo the tradition of showing up to the banquet at all and instead make love to my wife."

The following morning, as they slept in after a long night of enjoyment, they were interrupted by King Nilhist, who burst into their room, destroying the lock on the door. He was accompanied by Lyshyla, who was trying to calm him down, his guards, and the former bride-to-be, Onissa.

Prince Ozias sat up, speechless as he lay under the covers, naked with Oadira. Without a thought, Oadira conjured a blade under the sheets just in case King Nilhist's anger exploded into violence. She would not be caught off-guard, nude or not.

"This is unforgivable," King Nilhist shouted, seething with rage. "From this moment on, this sham of a marriage is null and void!"

"Father, my heart belongs to another," Ozias said in a stern voice.

"This is unforgivable," King Nilhist repeated, his rage boiling out. The muscles on his neck grew tighter with each word. "I say again, this marriage is null and void. Your deception has embarrassed your entire kingdom in the eyes of our allies, King Olit and Queen Ova, not to mention their daughter Onissa, who stands before you now forgiving and ready to wed you properly."

"It's too late, Father," Ozias said slowly.

"Nothing is too late!" Nilhist shrieked, spit flying from his lips. "As king, I deem this marriage annulled. As. Of. Now!"

"It cannot be, my former king," Lyshyla said, stepping forward.

"Former…King?" Nilhist questioned, eyes twitching. "Explain, before I have you removed from your station."

"According to the ancient laws passed down by Ishtar and Obatala," Lyshyla began as if teaching a class of children about proper etiquette. "As you know, Oadira is queen according to the Chosen Right of Election. The queen's Kemite bloodline superseded that of the current king and queen in power. Ozias has married a Black Madonna. Their marriage is consummated and therefor binding before the Educators and the gods of our ancestors. Power now resides within Oadira's Orishan bloodline."

Lyshyla looked at the couple still sitting naked in bed and grinned.

"Were you involved with this?" King Nilhist demanded, teeth grit. Sweat dripped from his forehead, eyes bloodshot.

"I was," Lyshyla said.

"Why?" King Nilhist asked.

"The Signs of the Times are upon us," Lyshyla replied. "And the Black Madonnas are the only ones that have the ability to stop what is coming. Your fear and paranoia have gotten the better of you."

Nilhist towered over Lyshyla, but she stood firm and unmoving. "The people won't accept this," he seethed. "I have been king for over 300 years. It is my right."

"It is the right of the Chosen Bloodline," Lyshyla corrected with a raised finger. "You may have hidden the records after the queen's death, but I am not the only one who knows the laws. And the people will accept the will of the gods over your will. I will make the proclamation as soon as we are done here, along with the other Educators and regents with whom I've already conferred this morning and tell the people of the blessed news; another Sign of the Times has come to pass. It's over, Nilhist. You are king no longer."

"How could you do this to me?" King Nilhist asked, turning to Ozias. He glared at Oadira and pointed. "You did this. You came here like a demon intent on taking my power."

Oadira sat tall, holding both to the sheet covering her nakedness and the hidden blade. "I came here to find a way back to Sahael for all our people. Solomon said this was the next step on my journey, and he was right. I don't care about being queen over your hidden city. I care about the man I love, and that he was prepared by the gods to help save millions of our people."

"Father, this is my choice, and I will have to live with the consequences of my actions," Ozias said.

"What do you have to say to your betrothed?" Nilhist asked, motioning to Onissa who stood silently behind the king. "She came here to take you back and forgive your indiscretions. And now you would spit on her kindness and generosity."

Ozias made eye contact with Onissa.

"My heart belongs to another. I'm sorry that I've embarrassed you," Ozias said.

Onissa put her nose up in the air and walked slowly out of the room.

"My king and queen, please get some rest," Lyshyla said, snapping her fingers at the startled guards standing next to the broken door. "When you both are ready, I'll see you in the pyramid. An escort will lead you there by sled. Come everyone, leave them alone. They need their space. We need to allow Ibeji to bless their bloodlines with children."

Nilhist, now a former king, walked out, shoulders slumped. His guards followed Lyshyla, leaving him to wander alone the halls that moments before had been his to rule.

Afterward while resting, King and Queen Ocnus ate their first meal as husband and wife. As the morning progressed, they dressed and followed their escorts to the sled that would take them to the caverns and the Pyramid of Iceoth. The journey was cold, but pleasant. By evening they had arrived and made their way down into the caverns where they met with Lyshyla. She was more than happy to see them and seemed excited to share the information she had found as she led them into the pyramid central chamber with its comfortable seating and floating yellow lights.

"I'm so glad you're here, your majesties. Shortly after the two of you were married, the writing on these Nivenor scrolls lit up," said Lyshyla, holding the parchments. "One of the Anubis Guards sent word to me as soon as it happened. I'd never read these scrolls before. They were piled with shipping manifests and old trade documents."

"Nivenor scrolls? What's in them?" Oadira asked, coming near Lyshyla, who handed her the rolled manuscripts.

"Nivenor scrolls contain information about your pedigree. These explain everything about the bloodline of the Orisha consisting of the Nephilim and the Negralli."

"What did you learn?" Ozias asked.

"You need to read them for yourself." Lyshyla pointed to the scrolls in Oadira's hand.

Oadira sat down at a table with Ozias and started reading the Nivenor scrolls for the next few hours. What they learned excited them as much as it had Lyshyla.

"I had no Idea there were over 250,000 Negralli that

married 250,000 Nephilim," Oadira said, taking a bite of whey bread Lyshyla had brought to them. "The remaining one billion Negralli were to be born and brought into Aarde through Nier's realm in the north as Orishan children through the Ancient Bloodline. They were to be Sahaelian inhabitants and the protectors of the Alkebulan people."

"It's exciting, isn't it?" Lyshyla said.

Oadira nodded. "Ishtar and Obatala married the kings and queens of the Chosen Bloodlines in secret for years before the actual festivities took place, just like Ozias and I did yesterday. It's amazing!"

"Exactly like the idea you, me, and Ossa came up with," Lyshyla said with a slight chuckle. "Please continue."

"Ishtar and Obatala in secret married multiple lineages. The Negraté and the Eloquimmian bloodlines, the Negrunde and the Anunnaki bloodlines, and lastly, the Egyptians and the Nelioan bloodlines. After the merging of these bloodlines, three more additional bloodlines were created, the Yoruba, the Hausa, and the Demir. It goes on to say that each bloodline was given a set of conditions to protect, unite Sahael with Egyptus, and serve the Alkebulan people at all costs. The Orisha, Yoruba, Hausa, and Demir bloodlines are directly related to the Watchers of the four realms, who also married in secret." Queen Oadira looked up from the scroll and then asked, "What does Nivenor's meaning of marriage in secret mean?"

"It means that the Watchers were married in similar fashion hundreds of years ago," Lyshyla answered. "What you two have done is no coincidence. I've been reading some of the related documents as well since you arrived. I didn't even know much of this, since the records weren't listed with the primary study resources of the Educator class here in Iceoth. Please listen as I retell to you the history written by Nivenor. You're going to be here for a while. I've arranged for more food to be brought to us," Lyshyla said with a smile.

"Tell us everything," Ozias said with a smirk. "But realize, at some point I'd like to spend some alone time with my wife. It is getting late at this point."

"You'll get your alone time," Lyshyla laughed. "But for now, let's dive in. After living and dwelling in Aarde for almost thirty years, the four Kemettian bloodlines combined with the four chosen lineages. The eight pedigrees bonded and emerged as four Ancient Bloodlines that formed into the four most powerful families in Sahael. The four lines of descent each produced a daughter through Ibeji's blessings. The four daughters were from the four Watchers realms, Nier's realm in the north, Neros's realm in the east, Nethal's realm in the west, and Naharis's realm in the south."

"I know this story," Oadira said. "The four baby girls were born without eyes."

"So, you know?" Lyshyla asked.

Oadira sat up, back straight. The words Solomon had told to her, Aamira and Heziara, came rushing back to her mind.

"I am one of those four baby girls who were born blind," Oadira said.

Silence reigned for a moment as all three of them pondered the implications of Oadira's admission.

"You were born without eyes?" Ozias asked, taking his wife's hand tenderly.

"I don't remember," Oadira said. "Solomon told me he gave me and the other three princess eyes of stone."

Lyshyla nodded, rubbing her chin thoughtfully. "Yes. The story goes that Ishtar and Obatala summoned Solomon who, with the help of the Kemite supreme leaders, Kaimana and Kanoa, helped Ishtar and Obatala's son provide sight to the four blind baby girls. Solomon, from where he stood, had the eight chosen families from Egyptus and Sahael place their babies on altars. Solomon pointed the baby girls in the directions of north, east, west, and south."

"Why?" questioned Oadira.

"To honor where the four baby girls had come from," Lyshyla said. "Solomon stood before each of the girls and made eight perfect balls of Orichalcum clay. He turned the balls into sapphires, emeralds, diamonds, and hematite. Solomon placed them into the empty eye slots of the four baby girls, providing them with eternal sight, power, and youth. Orichalcum mining was prohibited by the Kemites. It was carefully harvested until the Ancient Bloodlines were qualified to know how to use it for the benefit of the Sahaelian kingdom. Sahael was created and built on top of this Orichalcum. It's the most technological place in Aarde that we're aware of. We are in the Age of Discovery; they wanted to keep this knowledge away from the Narsans at all costs."

"Are they more powerful than the mothers who birthed them?" King Ozias asked. "Is Oadira stronger than the queens of Sahael I heard about as a child?"

"Yes, immensely," Lyshyla said.

"How is that possible?" he asked.

"Ishtar and Obatala blessed these precious stones with divine power and the ability to enhance their bloodlines and the bloodline of their offspring that would come from their wombs. Making it a decree, the Chosen Right of Election gives the chosen queens the right to bless any of the four Chosen Bloodlines that were pure. That came with the right to take over that bloodline and blessing the tribe and that lineage with ancient blood rights of power, gifts, freedoms, and eternal life," Lyshyla explained.

Oadira and Ozias looked at each other. Oadira thought of the responsibility placed upon her at that moment, now by extension, on Ozias as well.

Lyshyla motioned for them to follow her. They both got up and walked to an alcove at the end of the library. The lights followed overhead, casting shadows along the bookshelves as they walked. The space housed several tables covered in books along with wooden crates that held other documents and parchments.

"Over the last few weeks," Lyshyla said, "I have managed to compile drawings from the archives hidden for reasons beyond my understanding. I am sure in time the reasons will be revealed." She pointed to a wood engraving with a series of tall stones topped by other stones, each set forming what looked like a doorway. "These are depictions of Nairohenge Gates made out of Orichalcum transformed into obsidian rock," Lyshyla continued. "These gates lead to different locations throughout Aarde. These are what we've both been looking for, Oadira. This is the gate Solomon told you about, and what was spoken of in the documents you said were burned in the plantation fire."

"Who created them?" Ozias asked, running his finger along the grooves forming the image in the wood.

"Your people, the Kemites, created them as a means of protecting Black people all over Aarde. They also did it to protect themselves from the sun, prolonging their lives," Lyshyla said.

"Did the Kemites ever get to use them?" Oadira asked.

"Sparingly for travel, but never as a means of protection," said Lyshyla, looking over the pictures and reading the information. "Not much is said about the ancients. But at one point, they all lived in Sahael and Egyptus. They traveled throughout Aarde and built these gates everywhere."

"Is there a place that can provide more information about

all of this?" Ozias asked. "Maybe where the gates are located here in Iceoth?"

"I have been looking for a way to get back to a place that houses all knowledge in Aarde," Lyshyla said, placing the engraving back on the table with other sketches and documents. "The information that we have found here can help us understand the events that are happening around us. Once we understand why they are happening, we can understand what we all need to do next, and hopefully, where to go. For now, the two of you must make sure you are careful. Nilhist is upset about your marriage, and he may try to go out of his way to do something unexpected."

"I thought you said the people would fall in line and accept the ancient laws," Oadira said.

Lyshyla breathed deeply. "Yes, and I sent out the proclamations immediately after I left your quarters this morning. The response was not what I'd hoped. Many of the regents are on your side, but some of them are personally bound to Nilhist. If your father decides to fight back, I fear the people will be similarly divided. I thought the laws would be respected, but it seems our people have been apart from the rest of the world for too long. As I was leaving to come here, your father was whispering to one of his advisors, and I could tell it wasn't to cede the throne to you, Ozias. He feels betrayed, and I fear what he might do now that he sees himself pushed into a corner. The honorable man who I have followed since the day I arrived here with an Egyptian child seems to have fallen victim to his own fears. Things are not going as smoothly as I'd hoped."

"We should persuade the military to overthrow Nilhist if he doesn't abdicate the throne," suggested Oadira. "They'll be loyal to the rightful king, which is Ozias now."

"I agree," Ozias said. "I have as much sway with our generals as my father does. Plus, we have the Anubis warriors here. They only follow the ancient laws, so they will follow me."

"The Anubis warriors residing in the caverns should remain here to not frighten the people in the city," Lyshyla replied. "We must gain complete control of the military without going about it the wrong way. This is politics, something I am better trained in than you are, and yet still not as skilled as your father. If we want to avoid civil war, we may need to make some sort of deal with Nilhist."

"That is a big risk," Ozias said, smacking some of the papers on the table. "Nairobi law protects the former king from being killed by his army. If they remain loyal to him and I attempt to persuade them otherwise, they are within their right to have me executed without question."

"Then you must regain your father's trust so that he willingly hands military control over to you," said Lyshyla.

"I'm not sure that's possible," Ozias confirmed. "If the army stays loyal to him, he'll use it. He tried to make me marry a stranger and didn't tell me about it just to keep control. And what about the people? I've always been in the background for my father's dealings. They may not trust me to rule, in which case, we're in even more trouble. We may be in for a difficult time."

Oadira interlaced her fingers with Ozias'. "I can do difficult, so long as we're together."

Former King Nilhist seemed to grow even more bitter over the following months. He became constantly angry, and his anger seemed to age him. While the military had sided with Ozias, the people seemed to still consider Nilhist their leader. That being the case, the two men still needed to work together to keep some semblance of peace and normality in the kingdom, particularly since Dalean aggression had increased, as the flow of water to the western end of the continent had decreased. Many of the citizens of Benin saw Oadira as a temptress who had stolen the prince away from them, calling her names when she and Ozias walked outside the palace. She became an easy target of blame for the growing drought and any problems that sprung up in the city.

Complicating matters was the fact that after a spout of stomach flu that only seemed to affect her in the mornings, it became obvious Oadira was pregnant. she hadn't started to show yet, but within weeks that would no longer be the case. At Lyshyla's request, they kept the news between them, telling only Ossa as Ozias' best friend.

On a blustery morning, Oadira and Ozias entered the banquet hall hand-in-hand for their morning meal, seeing Nilhist hunched over the table eating mushy grains in a warm milk broth. He appeared to be in a dark mood.

"We have something to discuss, King of Benin," Nilhist said as he slurped.

"Yes, Father?" Ozias replied politely.

Nilhist sneered at Oadira. "Your bitch can go. This is between two kings, not a usurper."

Oadira leaned over slowly, looking Nilhist in his eye, staring until he glanced away in discomfort.

"I would defend my queen's honor," Ozias smiled, "but as you can see, it is unnecessary. She is the true ruler here, not you or I. But speak, Father. I have no wish for civil war, so let's please keep this civil."

"Civil," Nilhist snorted. "Poignant choice of words with the two of us on opposite sides of our kingdom's needs. I have a warning you need to take seriously. If a child is born between you and your consort, it would put our family and people in great danger."

"Why is that?" Oadira asked.

"Something you didn't think of when you set this in motion," Nilhist continued, slurping his mush once again. "The birth of a child would upset the balance of power among the tribes in Iceoth. We have scornful enemies because of your actions. They are looking to get revenge against the family."

"What are you talking about, Father?" King Ozias asked with a confused look on his face.

Nilhist slammed his spoon against the table. "Onissa, the woman you were supposed to marry, was involved with Lucedale colonial forces and their military general, Vipsanius. She and her parents sent a delegation yesterday warning they will reveal the location of Benin City and promising to destroy all the city's people if we don't acquiesce to their wishes."

"Father, how could you have let this happen?" Ozias asked. "You brought them here!"

"I had no choice," Nilhist spat. "The people were dying and in need of winter seed to place inside the icy ground. The harvests have been weak for the past year! I was looking for solutions to get crops to grow and fish to spawn in the lakes, streams, and rivers. I made a promise that if the Signs of the Times reached the shores of Iceoth, a marriage ceremony would have to take place in which a bride would come to Benin. When I made the promise, I had no idea the events would unfold the way they did."

"So, what do we do?" asked Ozias.

"Onissa and her family are beyond upset. They seek retribution for the embarrassment they suffered. For diplomatic reasons, you will be brought to stand before them, Ozias. Onissa's family does not recognize your marriage. Oadira was the woman you were forbidden to marry, and they knew it."

Oadira sat at the table and began tapping her finger against the granite surface. "There must be something we can offer to keep them from revealing Benin's location. Do they actually think the Dales will leave them alone if Benin falls? The witan governments will destroy them as---"

"Shut up, girl!" Nilhist screamed. "You know nothing of this! Commander Norg, Natas' right hand, has ordered General Vipsanius to execute Operation Red Dog. He plans to eliminate all the people living in the unclaimed lands in several places."

"Who is Norg?" Ozias asked.

"I know the name." Oadira replied slowly. "He is a military leader who was with Natas the night Sahael was destroyed."

"Yes," Nilhist said, body seeming to shrink in on itself the more he spoke. "He will do everything in his power to prevent her from returning there." He sat back and rubbed his forehead. "The Signs of the Times. The Signs of the goddamn Times."

"Does he know she's here?" Ozias asked; panic in his voice for the first time.

"Of course, he knows she's here!" Nilhist shouted. "Trade has halted between our kingdom and that of Olit's. Their anger is boiling over. They've told General Vipsanius that Oadira is here. They claim he's under Norg's command, which I don't doubt."

"So, Natas knows I'm here," Oadira breathed. Natas would stop at nothing to destroy Oadira, and he would slaughter anyone who stood in his way. Nilhist had every right to be worried and distraught.

"We don't know that," Ozias said, squeezing her hand.

"We do," Oadira replied, looking into his eyes. "If Norg knows, Natas knows." She turned to Nilhist. "Father-in-law, you and I have not been close from the moment we met. There has been a great deal of judgment and distrust on both sides. I know you were hurt by our deception on the wedding day, but you also knew what you were doing was wrong. Now we face a threat neither of us can handle alone. No single kingdom can handle it alone. It's time to give official control of the Anubis warriors to Ozias, along with the rest of the army."

"My warriors are loyal to Ozias as the lawful king under the Chosen Right of Election," Nilhist explained. "You know this already."

"But the people don't," Oadira said. "It's time this cold fight between all of us ends. Announce to the people that Ozias is the rightful king. Tell them he now has command of the legions as well as the Anubis Guard. Stand by his side as Steward of the Kingdom and let's fight our battles together. King Ozias will do the right thing. You've raised a strong Black man who will do what is right when the time calls for it."

Closing his eyes, King Nilhist nodded his head. "I'll never say you married a wilting flower, Ozias."

"I did not," Ozias chuckled.

"And I would keep no secrets from you, Lord Nilhist," Oadira said. She glanced at Ozias, who nodded his head, not needing to communicate telepathically to know what his wife meant by her statement. "I'm pregnant now, Father-in-law. Our bloodlines are joined. Whatever ties will be severed with Onissa and her tribe by this birth, let them be severed. They have already betrayed us, and their own people."

A slight smile spread across Nilhist's face. He glanced down at the table right where Oadira's stomach rested behind it. He nodded as a look of peace spread across his face.

"I will relinquish official control of the Anubis warriors," Nilhist said, pulling a golden, Ankh-shaped hilt from his belt. "I will then hand over control of Iceoth's military to both of you publicly." He reached over and put his hand on top of Ozias'. "Protect our people. Winter is coming on once again. The bays will freeze. That will be our only protection for the next few months. After that, armies from Dale may very well march on this city, allied with King Olit's forces of the Snow Canyon People. We must fight together."

Ozias nodded in agreement.

That afternoon a notification went out for the people to gather, so they could all see the transfer of power take place the following day.

Lyshyla officiated the proceedings as it was her responsibility to oversee all ceremonial engagements. King Ozias and his stepfather stood before the ice-stone throne and the people of Iceoth who were in attendance for the special ceremony.

Queen Oadira sat in one of the two thrones as Lyshyla addressed former King Nilhist and the current King Ozias Ocnus.

"We are all here today for the transfer of Iceoth's military power," she said, nodding to Nilhist. "The Anubis warriors are now under the direction and control of King Ozias."

Lyshyla handed Ozias the golden, Ankh-shaped hilt.

"The Anubis warriors will serve as Queen Oadira and King Ozias's personal guard," said Lyshyla.

The former king removed the dragon sapphire necklace from around his neck, walked up several stairs, and gave it to Lyshyla. King Ozias now had control of the Anubis army, and Queen Oadira had control of the Iceoth military.

"King Ozias Ocnus would now like to address you," Lyshyla said, ceding the platform to Ozias.

“People of Benin and greater Iceoth!” he shouted. “Today is a day of celebration. My father, King Nilhist, will remain by mine and Oadira’s side as our grand steward. We are united in all things, ready to face the future with steadfastness and grace. I thank my father now publicly for his support and wisdom. Blessed be Iceoth and the people of Benin.”

A cheer rose from the crowd as Nilhist waved and nodded to his son.

Lyshyla returned to her post as officiant on the platform, handing King Ozias the sapphire uraeus shaped like a dragon. After placing it around King Ozias’s neck, cheers filled the area, echoing throughout the city. Oadira sat on the throne as Ozias took his place next to her.

“Now we will seal the transfer of power from Steward Nilhist to the current king and queen,” Lyshyla shouted to the people. “I will recite the oath of protection for the people of Iceoth, a blood oath that must always be honored, no matter the circumstances. Both of you repeat after me: I, King Ozias and Queen Oadira, solemnly swear and affirm that we will support and defend the island of Iceoth against all enemies, foreign and native, and that we will bear true faith and allegiance to the same. We will obey the orders of Ishtar and Obatala and the orders of the kings, queens, emperors, empresses, and additional appointed titles of our ancestors.”

Oadira and Ozias recited every word after Lyshyla. With the ceremony complete, the celebration started.

There was joy and merriment, food and wine, dancing and singing as excitement swept through the city. Night came and the celebration ended, and the attendees fell asleep, filled with Amarula, the drink of choice throughout Alkebulan and now Iceoth.

Civil war had been averted.

But war was still coming.

Natas was coming, and nothing would keep him from his prize.

CHAPTER VIII

THE SINS OF MY FATHER

Iceoth, Benin City, City Palace

A brutal winter fell on Iceoth in the year 1519, far worse than any in a century. Benin was cut off from trade routes for six months. Luckily, the refugees that had followed Oadira and Ozias from the slave ships became the city's saving grace. Their work ethic and ability to persevere even in the most difficult circumstances allowed enough food to be produced to keep the kingdom from starving. Rationing became common by the third month of winter, but no one went without food. To Oadira's joy, even Steward Nilhist admitted the great blessing their coming had been to the people of Benin.

Peace reigned, and Oadira's pregnancy progressed. By the beginning of the thaw, the day of her delivery loomed. Sleeping had become difficult as every position she tried seemed less comfortable than the last. Her feet ached, her joints ached, even her teeth seemed to ache. Each morning she was ready for her pregnancy to end.

"It's official," Lyshyla said as she entered the royal chambers on the afternoon of the official spring thaw. "Onissa and her family have sold us out to the colonial forces who will be arriving on our shores any second now. The bays thawed fully last week, and word has reached me that ships of Narsan design, along with Dalean vessels, are massing near Solrin Ridge."

"Do we have a plan?" King Ozias said, looking up from the documents that he had been reading.

"Your father has a plan," Lyshyla answered. "Trust it. I have felt the change in his heart. Go along with whatever he has planned. And how are you feeling today, my queen?"

"Uncomfortable," Oadira joked, shifting in her chair and rubbing her enormous belly.

"Are our forces ready," Ozias asked, the only person in the room not smiling at Oadira's comment.

"As ready as they can be," Lyshyla nodded.

"Keep me informed. Dismissed."

Lyshyla bowed and walked out.

Is everything okay? Oadira asked Ozias telepathically.

I feel like I'm about to jump off a cliff, Ozias said.

You are king. Oadira asked. *The people are with you. Your father is with you. I am with you.*

And that is enough, King Ozias smiled. *How about we go for a walk under the Marula trees like we would when hiding from my father?*

"I'd like that," Oadira said out loud.

Oadira and Ozias prepared to leave when Oadira's stomach and back surged with sharp, intensifying pain. Her legs shook violently as clear fluid flowed down the inside of her legs. She stumbled, but Ozias caught her before she fell.

"Are you okay?" he asked in shock.

"The baby is coming—now!" Oadira said.

Ozias rushed her from the royal chambers, shouting for Ossa to join them. Running at full speed, Ossa appeared from around a corner and helped Oadira limp toward the birthing suite where all royal children were born among the purple tapestries of Ishtar. Another sharp pain tightened Oadira's stomach, and she cried out.

"Where are the midwives?" Ozias asked Ossa.

"They've been notified and will meet us at your chamber doors," Ossa said. "I'll make sure Lyshyla knows we're on our way there." He ran off again, grinning from ear to ear.

The midwives arrived quickly with Lyshyla and took Queen Oadira to the birthing chamber.

"I'll accompany the queen." Lyshyla said. "You wait outside until you're needed."

Queen Oadira was taken to her birthing chambers, in which there was a queen-sized bed. in the center of the room was a wooden pole made from the wood from the Marula Tree that stretched from the top of the ceiling to the floor. Purple tapestries hung from the walls. White feathers covered the floor to lessen the baby's impact after it was pushed out of Oadira's body.

Another contraction hit Oadira, and she thought she would fall over from the discomfort.

"Queen Oadira, you need to grab the wooden Marula pole," Lyshyla said, comfortingly. "The midwives are waiting for the baby to drop from your womb. They will help guide you through the entire process until the baby is born and then escort you to your bed. They will bring the baby to you after they finish bathing it, making sure it's clean and healthy." Lyshyla glanced toward the door where Ozias still stood, face pale. "King Ozias, you need to wait in the hall, as is custom."

"I'm not waiting out there! I want to see my child being born—to hell with the customs."

Just then, former King Nilhist walked into the doorway and grabbed his son by the arm. "You need to not be here. The longer you remain here, the greater the danger your wife and child face. You need to remove yourself from the birth chamber as soon as possible. We are at war, remember. Lyshyla…assign several guards to watch the door. My son and I will---"

Before Nilhist could complete his sentence, several guards rushed into the room, wearing not the garb of Benin, but the pale gray tactical gear of the Snow Canyon people. One of them pulled out a knife and held it against Nilhist's throat. One of the midwives screamed.

"What is the meaning of this?" Ozias shouted.

Onissa stepped into the birthing suite and stood next to her guards. Her long curly, brown hair fell over her shoulders. She had a hint of blue in her eyes and wore no royal cape, merely tactical gear like her soldiers. Two more guards entered and grabbed Ozias, forcing him to the floor.

"Ossa!" Ozias shouted "Ossa, we're under---"

One of the guards punched the king in his stomach, sending him pitching forward.

Oadira tried to stand, conjure a weapon, anything, but the pain of her delivery forced her to hold fast to the Marula pole. Sweat coated her skin. Would she die here, defenseless as she gave birth to her child? Lyshyla, as if sensing her fear, stepped in front of Oadira for protection.

"You will not harm her," Lyshyla cried.

"Or what?" Onissa asked. "You'll get me drunk again? Throw me into a servant's room until I sober up? You shamed me, that night, Lyshyla. I played the naïve princess thinking that's what you wanted me to be for Ozias, and you betrayed me."

"You dare enter the sacred birthing chamber?" Nilhist asked forcefully, neck exposed to the warrior's blade. "You dare attack my son, the king?"

"I am Onissa of the Snow Canyon People of Iceoth," Onissa cried, a madness to her eyes. "I am the woman you were supposed to marry, King Ozias. I have come with orders to take the life of Queen Oadira and any children that should come from your union." Onissa crouched next to Ozias as he struggled against her guards. "What does the king have to say for himself? Oadira's presence has signaled the Signs of the Times. The currents have brought death and danger to Iceoth's shores. Bring him to his knees!" The guards obeyed, pulling Ozias to his knees to face Onissa. "What will it be?" asked Onissa, looking past Ozias directly at Oadira. "Should I kill your father first, or your queen?"

"How did you know Oadira was going into labor?" Ozias grimaced.

"My spies alerted me days ago that the birth was close. Even in the palace among your regents there is dissension and fear of your bloodline. I was led inside this palace yesterday by your trusted servants to lie in wait with my guards. I heard the cry of Oadira's delivery with my own ears at it went through the palace." Onissa stood and pointed at Oadira. "We need to kill him and his family right now."

Despite the pain, Oadira focused on the pretty princess with her massive guards. No matter what, this daughter of Sahael would not go down without a fight. Her mother had died to protect her, and Oadira would die protecting her own child if needed. No one would harm that baby either before or after it was born.

Ozias struggled, staring at Onissa. "If you do this now, then all is lost, leaving no hope for Sahael. I don't know what the future holds. But I have read the inspiring histories of our people. The histories of the Orishas and the Oralian's, the exiled bloodline. The two are the same. They share the same bloodline. They are one tribe! We are one tribe!"

"Enough of this nonsense," said Onissa, smirking. "Those histories are not true and are nowhere to be found inside that cavern."

"How would you know?" King Ozias asked.

"Because I've been there," Orissa smiled. "You think you're the only ones who can access the archive? That no one could ever get passed your Anubis Guards? My father found the entrance long ago. He infiltrated the archives. Your mother found out about it one night, but my father forced the collapse of the caverns with his ice bombs, killing her."

"No!" Nilhist shouted. "It was an accident that killed her!"

"Think what you will," Onissa said, slapping Nilhist's face. "My father takes great pride in the act that put King Nilhist on the path of insanity. And now his bloodline ends."

Nilhist stood up straighter, looking from the guard holding the knife to his neck and back to Onissa. "Ozias is not of my bloodline."

Odira listened through the pain, wondering what Nilhist was playing at.

"There was a section of the Orishan people who broke off from the Chosen Bloodline because they chose to live outside of Sahael," King Nilhist said. "These Oralian's chose to live in Iceoth, a barren, uninhabitable land made livable as a place of refuge. It was considered a break off to preserve the Orishan bloodline. It was an order given by Nygaard, the first Oralian king, who prophesied that a virgin would arrive on the shores of Iceoth. The virgin's arrival was to signal a changing of the times, signifying a return home to Sahael. That virgin was Oadira, a

Black Madonna. King Nygaard prophesied and promised the Madonna's children would unite Sahael and the Sahaedron Kingdom. At first, I thought her a curse, but now I know she is the blessing."

"What do you mean, I'm not of your bloodline, Father?" Ozias asked.

"I am not your father," Nilhist said, head dropping slightly. "You were brought here by Educator Lyshyla for your own protection. We took you in and adopted you."

Ozias' face seemed to melt as it drooped. "You're not…and Mother wasn't…"

"Your birth mother was of this Orishan remnant, as was your father," Nilhist continued, "which is why you and Oadira have abilities I do not share. I'm sorry I never told you."

So that was it. More secrets. More revelations. More lies coming out.

"Being in a royal court is always exciting, Isn't it, Ozias?" Onissa smirked.

Ozias stopped struggling and bowed his head. He then looked at Onissa. "Princess Onissa, I ask that you forgive me for my actions. I am in love and have always been in love with Queen Oadira from the moment our eyes met on the discarding ships. I am sorry for what you suffered on our wedding night. I don't know whether it's true your father killed my mother or not, but there is no need for more blood to be shed. Your people are in danger just as the people of Benin. The Narsans and Dales won't be content to destroy and enslave us. They will come for you next."

"Let them come," Onissa spat. "As long as your line is ended, I will die content. Kill the queen first. Cut that bastard from her belly and I'll kill it myself."

Hearing those words gave Oadira the strength she needed.

The pain of the contractions disappeared. She stood, forming a glowing blade in each hand. With a flick of her wrist, she sent the knives flying. They both hit the guards holding Ozias in the back. They screamed in pain, releasing him. Nilhist, taking advantage of the confusion, grabbed the knife from his assailant's hand and plunged it into the man's own neck. Lyshyla rushed forward as well, grabbing one of the guards Oadira had stabbed and snaping his neck, while Ozias crushed the windpipe of the other.

Onissa turned to run, just as Ossa entered the birthing chamber brandishing a sword.

"My king!" Ossa cried, running into Onissa and knocking her to the floor. "Steward Nilhist! Snow Canyon soldiers tried to surround the palace as you predicted, but the Anubis Guard overpowered them. Your orders for them to be on alert averted disaster."

"You knew?" Ozias said as he released the now dead guard. "This was your plan?"

"My plan was for us to get farther away from the birthing chamber before Onissa found us," Nilhist admitted. "Go, check on your wife. We can discuss my failed plans later."

Ozias stood and ran over to Oadira as she collapsed back against the Marula pole. "Are you alright, my love?" he said, caressing her face.

"I'm okay," Oadira smiled. "I just want to get this baby out of me now."

Nilhist lifted Onissa from the floor, holding her up so her feet didn't touch the ground.

"What are you going to do? Kill me?" Princess Onissa asked.

"We are not going to kill you," Nilhist replied. "That would force a civil war with the Snow Canyon Peoples. I will reach out to your father and mother, and they will know of your shame this day. I knew you were in the palace. That is why I tried to lead Ozias away from the birthing suite. I thought it would take longer for you to find us and that by then my guards would have arrived at the door. Still, thanks to Oadira and the Anubis Guard, your little assault failed before it could begin."

King Ozias gagged Princess Onissa, preventing her from speaking any more, and tied her arms and feet, so she couldn't run away.

"What are we going to do with her?" Ozias asked.

Nilhist reached down in his pocket and grabbed a whistle, blowing a high-pitched, airy sound of a bird mixed with a growl. He then handed the whistle to Ozias.

"What is this?" Ozias asked.

"Watch and observe," Nilhist said, pointing toward the balcony overlooking the city below.

Oadira looked out over the balcony and spotted a group of beautiful, half-bird and half-woman sirens with shimmering, black-walnut skin. They each had long black braided hair, shiny, white teeth, and majestic wings.

"Are those sirens?" Ozias asked.

"Yes," Nilhist confirmed. "It's called the Lover's Whistle; a trinket a siren bestows on the man they fall in love with. They heard your mother's song deep within the ice canyons. You're about to meet Ujana, queen of the sirens, and your grandmother."

Two sirens remained flying just beyond the balcony, while the center woman, dressed in shiny white and gold robes, stepped into the chamber from the outside.

"Who summons us using my daughter's whistling voice?" Ujana, queen of the sirens, said.

“It is I who has summoned you,” Nilhist said.

“Why have you summoned me and my flock here?” Queen Ujana asked. “You have not used the whistles since the death of my daughter, Queen Nilda.”

“I have a young child that requires safety and exile,” former King Nilhist said.

“Show me the child,” Ujana said, clinging to the rail with her talons.

“This woman,” Nilhist said, gesturing to Onissa, who was bound and gagged. “She has lost her way and sold-out her people to the colonial forces who will be arriving on the Iceoth shores soon. Princess Onissa is a threat to my adopted son, your grandson. If she remains, my grandchildren and your grandchildren will have to look over their shoulders forever. They will never be safe.”

“I understand,” Queen Ujana said, ordering her flock to take Princess Onissa away from the palace.

Ujana looked at King Ozias. “It is good to meet you, grandson. Your mother loved you and did everything for you, even making the hardest sacrifice a mother could ever make for her child. As will I. All you need to do is call on us, and we will hear you.” She then glanced over at Oadira. “May Sahael rise once more with the power of the Chosen Bloodline.”

Queen Ujana spread her wings and lifted off the balcony, flying from their presence. Ujana grew smaller as she drifted from Oadira’s sight.

“How is Oadira?” Nilhist asked, turning from the balcony.

“I’m alright,” Oadira groaned as Lyshyla rushed to help her stand against the pole to continue the birth.

“You should both go,” Lyshyla said. “Have the guards posted as planned, but now we need to help Oadira. None of us was planning on an assassination attempt before the birth."

Ozias nodded and stepped toward the door with Ossa. Nilhist grabbed his arm.

"I apologize for giving you so much resistance regarding Oadira," Nilhist said, voice eager. "I apologize for forcing you into a situation where you had to marry your love in secret. The events of Nygaard's prophecy are being fulfilled right before our eyes. Your mother and I wanted a life for you that didn't involve you worrying about what was happening to Black men being enslaved in Aarde and the additional and external challenges you also would have to deal with as a Black man in Aarde. Your mother and I wanted you to grow up and raise children away from the threat of enslavement. I promised your mother before she died that I would do everything in my power to protect you. I have failed her. I may not be your natural father, nor did your late mother give birth to you, but I always felt like we were, and so did she. Neither of us could ever bear to tell you. But now the truth must come out." He nodded to Oadira. "I accept the truth."

Ozias hugged his stepfather. They both looked over the balcony once more.

"What will you tell the Snow Canyon People about their princess?" King Ozias asked.

"I'll deal with that when the time comes," former King Nihilist said. "I will prepare Iceoth's defenses and make sure the people that need protection have it, including the increasing number of Alkebulan refugees entering Benin City. They are worthy of our city. I'm sorry I didn't see that before."

"You are forgiven," Odira breathed. "Now get out so I can have this baby!"

I love you, Ozias said telepathically as he walked out. *See you and our child soon.*

I love you too. Go help our people.

Ozias and Nilhist walked out to face a war right on their doorstep.

TO BE CONTINUED

www.ingramcontent.com/pod-product-compliance
Lightning Source LLC
Chambersburg PA
CBHW010448310726
48979CB00018B/2856/J

* 9 7 8 1 9 6 3 0 8 9 0 1 1 *